Finding
Daniel

NANCY C. COMPTON

ISBN 978-1-64670-650-1 (Paperback)
ISBN 978-1-64670-651-8 (Digital)

Covenant Books, Inc.
11661 Hwy 707
Murrells Inlet, SC 29576
www.covenantbooks.com

CONTENTS

CONTENTS

CHAPTER 1
Daniel's Kidnapping

Binghamton Press/Sun Bulletin
July 31, 1990

Kidnapping in Owego, New York

The police report that on July 30, 1990, Daniel Kenneth Leonard was kidnapped from his grandparents' home by his uncle and taken to an undisclosed place. Daniel's parents are Christine Taber and Ken Leonard, both of Owego. The police have arrested Christopher Taber and have charged him with kidnapping. He is being held in the Tioga county jail until he is placed in a facility for the mentally handicapped. The baby's grandparents are Carol Anne and Dan Taber and James and Elizabeth Leonard. Anyone that knows the whereabouts of baby Daniel is asked to contact the New York State Police with any information about him.

This was not the way their lives were supposed to be. They were in school. Ken was going to Harvard, and Christine was attending SUNY-Binghamton. They had planned on getting their educations and then getting married, but that was not the case for them.

They had grown up in Owego, New York, a small town on the banks of the Susquehanna River. Their families had always lived in Owego, and they were connected socially. Dan Taber, Christine's father, was a businessman, and his grandfather Jonathan Taber had been a close friend of John D. Rockefeller; and together, they had started the Standard Oil Company. They had been school friends. John D. had grown up in a small town north of Owego called

Rockford. Jonathan amassed much wealth with his investments into the oil company, and the family was very well off. They lived in a large mansion just west of the center of town.

Ken's family was also in the same social circle that the Taber family traveled in. James Leonard was a self-made man. He had also attended Harvard and graduated top of his class form the Harvard Business School. He was much sought-after and finally decided to take a job just half an hour from where he had grown up. He worked in a company in Endicott, New York and had grown with the company and now was the CEO of National Computer Technologies.

The kidnapping was a great tragedy for both families, and all the money that they both possessed could not bring Daniel back to his family.

As the years went by, the families continued to look for Daniel. During those years, many things happened that his family wished he was there for, but he was not. His father graduated from Harvard Business School, top of his class, and was working for National Computer Technologies with his father. Ken and Christine had gotten married now and have two more children, Alyssa and Trent. They were a happy family and had wonderful times together; but there was always a dark cloud hanging over Ken and Christine, who always felt the loss of Daniel.

Every year on Daniel's birthday, the families would have articles run in the newspapers about the kidnapping, along with Daniel's baby picture, but no one ever contacted the state police with a reported sighting. As Daniel's twentieth birthday approached, Christine decided that she had to give it at least one more try. She had an artist do a picture of what Daniel might look like at age twenty. This, along with one of his pictures at age two months, would be put in the article they could run in the newspapers up and down the East Coast. They were going to flood the papers with the article and had hopes that someone would know Daniel as an adult and let them know about him.

In preparing the article for the newspapers, Christine had heard about a newspaper that was published in the Amish community in Ohio and decided to give it a try. *The Budget* was published once a month, but it had a large circulation.

CHAPTER 2

Daniel's Life in Lancaster, Pennsylvania

In Lancaster County, Amos and Mary Lapp had just been in the doctor's office where they were told that Mary would not be able to have any more children. They already had five but longed for more to complete their family. As they made their way home, Amos talked to her, saying that the doctors weren't always right, and they would check with another one. "We can always adopt. There are lots of children that need a good home with loving parents and brothers and sisters to play with." They stopped to do some shopping and enjoy the spring weather. "Summer will be here soon."

As they started down Belmont Road, a car with New York license plates came toward them. Tourists didn't come down their road very often. "Maybe they are lost," Amos said.

They had pulled into their drive, and Amos stopped the buggy near the back door so they could unload their purchases. The children were at Mary's sister's house while they went to the doctor's. Stepping out of the buggy, Mary thought that she heard a cat crying. Listening closer, she knew it was a baby crying. "Do you hear that?" she asked Amos. "It sounds like a baby."

They took their packages from the buggy and walked to the porch. "Someone has left a basket on our porch."

As they got close enough to see in the basket, they were stopped in their tracks. There was a baby in the basket. Mary walked up the steps and took a closer look. The baby appeared to be a couple of months old. "Open the door, Amos. We need to get this baby in the house where it is warmers."

Amos took Mary's bags from her hands and unlocked the door while she picked up the basket and took it into the kitchen. "I think he is hungry. Can you put some milk in a pan to warm?"

She reached into the basket to pick the baby up. It was a precious child, so beautiful. In the basket, she found a diaper and took the baby into their bedroom to change it. She picked up the baby. She found an envelope under the blanket.

As she bent to pick it up she said to Amos, "Look at this." Opening it, she read the note aloud. "Please take care of my baby. I can't take care of him, and he needs to be loved and taken care of. He needs to grow up in a loving home. His name is Daniel. Raise him as your own, but don't tell him that he was left on your porch. Thank you."

"What do you make of that?"

"I guess someone decided they couldn't raise this child. What should we do?" Mary asked.

"We need to get in touch with the authorities and turn this baby over to them," Amos replied.

"No! We need to talk about this. The note asked us to take care of this child. Why can't we raise him as our own. We can say we adopted him. He was left on our doorstep because the Lord knows how we long for another child."

"We can't say we adopted him. Someone will find out, and we could be in a lot of trouble. The children will start talking about a new baby at their house, and then what will happen?"

"We can tell the members of our family that the doctor arranged it, and we can tell the doctor we went through an agency. This is our chance to add to our family," Mary said with so much emotion, Amos decided she was right.

Mary fed the baby and put him in the basket to sleep. She had to find all the things that she had put away from the children. She had to wash and clean them so the baby would have something to wear. The crib was stored in the shed, so Amos found and empty drawer to use as a bed for the baby for tonight. He found a piece of foam to fit the drawer, and he put a big towel over that.

Before Amos and Mary went to bed that night, Mary fed Daniel again and put him in the drawer to sleep. Mary didn't sleep much that night, thinking about everything that they would need for the new addition to their family.

In the morning, over breakfast, Mary said, "We will need to buy some baby things. We need new bottles, diapers, clothes, soap. Well, just everything."

"Yeah, we will go first thing after chores."

Once they had eaten breakfast and were done with the morning chores, they were on their way to buy the things they needed for Daniel. "We need to get him some clothes. Let's go to Walmart. That is the best place to buy the things we need for him now. When he gets bigger, I will make his clothes."

When they returned home that night, they had everything they could think of that they would need for Daniel. They had stopped at Mary's sister's house to pick up the children, and everyone was excited about the new baby.

Daniel fit into the family easily. He was a cute little guy. Mary and Amos's families were so happy when they found out about the baby. Daniel was loved by everyone in the family. He was a lovable little guy.

Mary and Amos's oldest child was David. After David came Samuel, Annie, Kate, and Rebecca. Mary and Amos had always made it clear that Daniel was an adopted son. Even though he was adopted, his coloring was like the rest of the children: light-brown hair and blue eyes.

The Lapp family were a loving family, and the children grew up having a wonderful childhood. They all looked up to their parents. They attended the same one-room schoolhouse and had lots of friends. It was a wonderful time in the life of the Lapp family.

CHAPTER 3

Visiting Lancaster

Ken's mother had been Amish when she was growing up. That had always fascinated Ken. Because of his connection to the Amish community, Ken and Christine decided to go to visit the Lancaster area for a long weekend. The first weekend in October found the Leonard family on their way to Lancaster. Ken had done his research and found a place called the Fulton's Steamship Inn for them to stay in. He liked the location and decided that they would stay there. It was located on the corner of Route 30 and Hartman Bridge Road that leads to Strasburg.

They traveled around the area experiencing the Amish community. They went on a buggy ride, toured the Amish house and farm, and ate at the Amish restaurants. This was a wonderful experience learning about the life that his mother and her family had lived at one time.

One of the places they stopped at was the Amish Cupboard. All the men were Amish craftsmen, and they made furniture and custom-made cabinets. Ken's grandfather owned a business that made custom made cabinets and furniture. He had been in the custom furniture when he and his wife left the Amish fold. He started a business that only employed Amish men, and they did fine work. It had grown so much that they had several hundred workers in three locations in the United States. The main one was in Owego, New York, not far from the Amish community in Troy, Pennsylvania.

While at the Amish Cupboard, Christine was fascinated by the wonderful workmanship in the products they were making. She thought about her husband's grandfather's work and was happy to see that it was almost as good. She stood and watched a young Amish man working on a table. There was something about him that drew her to watch; there was something about him that was familiar. It was as if she had known him all her life, but that was impossible.

Daniel helped his father around the farm, along with his brother, but his calling was woodworking. He had a good job at the Amish Cupboard where they made fine furniture pieces. He loved to take a piece of wood and make it into a fine work of art.

He had a strange feeling today at work. A family came into the store, looking at the furniture. The mother stopped at the window and watched him for a long time. Something about the woman drew him. He couldn't explain it. As he worked, he would look out of the corner of his eye at her. What was it about this woman that kept his interest and made him think about her long after she had gone.

The family soon left; and a few days later, he had forgotten all about her.

CHAPTER 4

Daniel's Twentieth Birthday

In Owego, Christine was busy sending out pictures of Daniel as a baby and an enhanced picture of what he might look like at age twenty. She was sending these pictures to newspapers all over, just on the slim chance that someone would recognize him. She included her name, address, and phone number. Also, in the article, it told that Daniel had a birthmark on his wrist.

As she prepared the information for the newspapers, she couldn't help but look at the enhanced photo of Daniel and think about how much he looked like Ken at that age. Maybe he really does look like his father. On May 25, Daniel's pictures appeared in over one hundred newspapers in New York, Pennsylvania, and down the East Coast.

Christine waited to hear from someone, but she didn't get even one call. The one last newspaper that would not come out until the end of May was the Amish newspaper *The Budget*. She was still hoping for a call coming, but there was very slim hope.

* * * * *

In Lancaster, Daniel was thinking about his upcoming birthday. He was not married and didn't even have a girlfriend. It didn't bother him. He was saving his money for the day when he would have a wife and family to support. He would want to be able to continue his woodworking and had thoughts about someday having his own business. That was a long way in the future, though.

Amos was heading home after doing some errands and stopped to pick up a copy of *The Budget*. When he arrived home, it was just as dinner was ready. After lunch, he went to work in the fields with his sons, so it wasn't until after supper that he had time to sit down and read *The Budget*.

As Amos read, there were several humorous stories and sad stories; but turning the page, he found himself looking at a picture of Daniel. There was an article that told about the story of Daniel's kidnapping when he was two months old, and that he was never found. In the article was a name, address, and phone number if anyone had information about this young man. "Mary, come here and look at this," Amos said.

"Did you find something interesting?" she asked. As Mary approached Amos he turned the paper around so Mary could see the article and picture. She was shocked. She took the paper and sat down to read it. "We have to show this to Daniel. This is from his parents. Amos, those poor people. Their son was kidnapped. All these years, they have been searching for him. We have had our wonderful boy all this time, and now his family needs to know him."

"How will we explain that he wasn't adopted properly? What will the people think when they find out that he was left on our porch in a basket? We have raised a fine young man as our own with love and understanding."

Mary said, "I know how I felt when we found him on our porch. I was so happy. I never thought that maybe someplace, someone was looking for their kidnapped son. That makes me sad. What we need to do now is to help Daniel to connect with his biological parents."

They sat there for several minutes thinking. Amos finally agreed with her that they needed to show the article to Daniel as soon as he came in.

The house was silent, just the ticking of the clock. Finally, the back door opened, and there was a loud stomping of feet in the mudroom. The door to the kitchen finally opened, and in came Daniel with a big smile. "Hey, what's up? You look like something terrible has happened."

"Daniel, come down, we have something to show you. There is an article in *The Budget* that you need to see," Amos said as he handed the paper to him.

Daniel looked at the pictures first. "How did they get this picture of me? I never saw anyone taking a picture head on."

"It is a picture that they call enhanced to show what someone would look like older than what they were when they were last photographed. The police use this a lot to find missing persons."

Next, Daniel read the article. When he was done reading, he read it again. This time, when he was finished reading, he looked at his parents. "What do I do?" he asked.

"The final decision is up to you, but we both think you should contact this family. Can you imagine how they have felt all those years ago when you were kidnapped? Not knowing where you were. Always wondering if their child was even alive. We will stand behind you whatever your decision is," Amos told his son.

That night, Daniel didn't sleep much. He wondered what his parents were like. He knew, at least he was pretty sure, that they were not Amish. How would they feel when they found out that he was. Where did they live? The article said Owego, New York, but where was that? Should he write a letter or call from the phone shed? So many questions, so few answers.

The next morning Daniel was in the barn when his father came in. Amos looked at his son and saw that he had not slept well last night. He asked, "Did you sleep well last night?"

"I had a lot to think about. I have so many unanswered questions. I don't want to hurt you and mother, but I am curious about my parents. Should I write them, or should I call?"

"We don't want to lose you, but we have had you for twenty years, twenty years that your parents have been looking for you. I can't imagine what it must have felt like when they discovered that you were gone. Why don't you call the number in the paper?"

"If you think it won't upset mother, I will later today."

Amos and his son finished their chores and went in to breakfast. Once Daniel washed up and sat down at the table, he looked at his mother. She looked tired. Had she slept well, or did she lay awake like he did? "Are you okay, son?" she asked.

"I'm fine. How are you? I am going to call the number in the article. This doesn't mean that I love you any less. I just need to find out if I am the son these people lost so many years ago."

"I think that is a wise decision."

Breakfast was a busy time, but Daniel's mother always had a wonderful spread of food, ham, eggs, toast, apple butter, cinnamon rolls fresh out of the oven, and much more.

At 11:00 a.m., Daniel entered the phone shed to make a call that would probably change his life forever. After dialing the number, he waited for someone to answer. When the phone had rung for the fourth time, he was ready to hang up when someone answered. "Hello."

"Hello, is this Mrs. Leonard?" Daniel asked.

"Yes, it is."

"Mrs. Leonard, I saw the article in *The Budget* about your son. I may be the person you are looking for. I look just like the enhanced picture that the police created, and I was adopted. I am twenty years old, and there was a note when my parents found me on their doorstep, saying that my name is Daniel. My parents kept that name."

"Wow, it sounds very promising. I have been searching for twenty years for our son. Where do you live, Daniel?"

"I live outside Strasburg, Pennsylvania. I am Amish."

"Is there anything else you would like to tell me?" Christine asked.

"Yes, I also have a birthmark. It is located just above my wrist on my left arm. It is shaped like a heart. I know that the article mentioned a birthmark, but it didn't say where. So I wanted to mention it. It may not be in the location of the one your son had."

"We deliberately did not put the location of the birthmark so that I would know if we might have the right person. I guess now all that is left is for us to come to Strasburg and meet you and your family. I will make arrangements to come to Strasburg tomorrow. I am not sure if my husband will be able to get away on such short notice, but I will be there. Is there a number that I can reach you at?"

"We have a phone, but it is in the shed. You can call and leave a message if no one answers. You can leave the number where you are, and I will call you when I am able."

"I will be staying at the Historic Strasburg Inn. We always stay there when we are down there visiting."

"Thank you, Mrs. Leonard. I look forward to meeting you." After Daniel hung up the phone, he headed to the barn so he could tell his father about the conversation.

In Owego, Christine hung up the phone and sat down. She couldn't believe the call she had waited twenty years for had finally come. She had to make sure that she did not get her hopes up. It may turn out that Daniel was not their son, but she was hopeful. After she was able to compose herself, she called Ken at work. "Ken, I just had a call from a young man that may be our son."

"Wait a minute. What did you say?"

"He told me that he had seen the pictures and the article in *The Budget*, and that he looks just like the enhanced photo that the police created. He lives outside Strasburg, and he is Amish. He was adopted, and he has just turned twenty years old. The one thing that just really made me stop and take notice was that he has a birthmark just above his wrist. He said that he wasn't going to call because the article did not say where the birthmark was, but he decided that he should in case he was our son. Oh! the birthmark is heart shaped."

"Do you really think it is him.?"

"I will find out tomorrow. Can you go down with me?" she asked.

"I can't. You go and talk to this young man. Then we will go from there. We don't want to rush into anything. Once we are sure, we will tell the family."

Once they had said their goodbyes, Christine headed up to their bedroom to pack. All the time she was packing, she was thinking about her conversation with Daniel.

CHAPTER 5
Christine Travels to Lancaster

The next morning, Christine got her family off to school and work, cleaned up the kitchen, and headed to the Lancaster area. Today, the drive seemed to take forever. At 3:00 p.m., she arrived at the inn. Once she was settled into her room, she called the Lapp phone shed.

While she was waiting for a callback, Christine unpacked her things. Still waiting for a call, she decided to go to the Strasburg Corner Store and Creamery for a quick bite to eat, stopping at the desk to give them her cell phone number so when Daniel called, they could give him the number.

After walking around the store and creamery, Christine headed back to the Inn. As she entered her room, the phone started ringing. "Hello, this is Christine Leonard."

"Mrs. Leonard, this is Daniel. Did you have a good trip?"

"Yes, Daniel, I did. Would it be possible for you to meet with me today?" she asked.

"My mother wants me to ask you to dinner. Dinner would be with my parents and my brothers and sisters. After dinner, we will be able to talk. If I am our son, I want you to see the kind of life I have had. Would you come to dinner?"

"Yes, Daniel, what time should I be there?"

"At 5:30 p.m. would be good."

"Okay, I will be there at 5:30. Tell me how to get to your home."

"When you leave the inn, turn left onto Route 896 and go to the corner of Route 896 and Route 741. Turn left onto Route 741, which is Strasburg Road. Stay on Route 741 until you get to Black

Horse Road. Turn left onto Black Horse Road to Quarry Road. Turn right onto Quarry Road. Our farm is the only house on that road. We will see you shortly. My parents are very anxious to meet you. Me too."

Christine only had a short time to freshen up and change her clothes. She wore a simple white blouse and black pants. She left with plenty of time to get to the Lapp farm if she got lost. Not to worry, though, Daniel's directions were very easy to follow, and she arrived right on time. Amos Lapp came out to the car to welcome her. "Welcome to our home. We are pleased to have you."

"Thank you, Mr. Lapp. I appreciate your hospitality. I have not come here to pull your family apart, just to find my son. If he is not interested in having a relationship with us, I will just know that he is well and has had a good life with you and your family."

"Please, call me Amos. Come in and meet my family and Daniel."

"I have to tell you that I am very nervous," Christine said.

As they entered the kitchen, Christine saw a woman and a young man standing together. Her eyes instantly went to Daniel. Two things struck her. First, she was amazed how much Daniel looked like the police enhancement; she remembered Daniel saying that when he called. Second, he looked just like Ken did at that age.

Amos introduced Christine to Mary and Daniel. As he finished, the rest of the family showed up and were introduced. Mary served a wonderful meal that night. Roast chicken, mashed potatoes, gravy, coleslaw, green beans, bread, butter, and apple butter. Conversation was light during the meal. Christine told them about Owego, where she had lived all her life. She told them about her two other children and Ken. They asked questions about her life and what New York was like.

When the meal ended, the girls were asked to clean the kitchen while they went into the front room to talk. Amos asked the first questions. "What happened when your child was taken?"

"My son was about two months old. I had given him his bottle and put him down for a nap. A short time later, I went to check on him, but I didn't find him in his crib. I looked through the house, but he was not there.

"My mother was on the patio, and I went to her and told her that I couldn't find Daniel. We both searched the house from top to bottom, but the baby was gone. We immediately called Ken, the baby's father, and my father and they both rushed to the house. We then called the police, and that started the investigation.

"What we didn't know at the time was that my twin brother wasn't around either. My twin, Christopher, has some problems. Every so often, he would take off in his car and would be gone for several weeks. We knew that this was a pattern with Chris, so we didn't think too much about him being gone.

"When the police were searching the house, they found a note in the baby's crib under the blanket from Chris. It said that he had taken the baby to someone who deserves him, and that he had taken him away from Owego, and I would never find him.

"The police searched for Chris's car but never found it. He appeared at home after several weeks. He was questioned by my father and then by the police, but he would not tell anyone where he had taken Daniel. As I said, Chris has problems and is now in a mental institution and will be there for the rest of this life.

"Our families went on with our lives. When Daniel's father graduated from college, we were married and now have two other children, Alyssa and Trent.

"We have never stopped looking for Daniel. Every year around his birthday, we would contact different newspapers and have them put an article in about the abduction. This year, we decided to flood the papers. We must have contacted some three hundred major publications, *The Budget* being one. We have had a wonderful life, but there was always a sadness because we had lost our son."

"That must have been terrible. Let us tell you about how we got Daniel. The day we found him on our porch, we had been to the doctors and found out that we would not be able to have any more children. We were upset. When we got home, we heard what we thought at first was a cat crying, but it wasn't. We found a baby in a basket on our porch. When we took him into the house, we found the note."

With that, Mary reached down and picked up a basket that had several items in it. "I have kept these things. These were the clothes Daniel had on when he came to us." She pulled out the clothes.

Christine sucked in her breath. That was the outfit that her Daniel had worn that day. "Oh my, that is what Daniel was wearing the day he disappeared." Christine started to cry softly. "I have to ask to see the birthmark," she said.

Daniel got up and walked to where Christine was sitting. Turning his arm, he displayed the mark.

"We have looked for you for so long. We never gave up hope that we would find you. Now that I see you and see where you have been all these years, I am comforted that you have been loved and well taken care of."

Turning to Amos and Mary, she said, "Thank you. I am so grateful to you for the love you've given to Daniel. I had hopes that I would find our son, and we would take him home, but I would never do that to you. I know you have cared for him as your own. Maybe someday, he will come up to New York for a visit."

"I don't know how I would be accepted in your town. I would feel very much out of place."

"I understand that. My mother-in-law was Amish when she was growing up. Her father left the community when he had a direct order from the elders that he could not use electricity for his livelihood. So he left the community and moved his family and his business to Owego, New York.

"Her father, Jacob King, is still living and has always stayed close to the Amish ways. He started a woodworking business in Troy, Pennsylvania. His company makes the highest quality Amish furniture, and he has been very successful. He employs only Amish woodworkers or former Amish. He has factories in three locations and employs over five hundred people. If he pulled into your drive now, you would think he was still a member of an Amish community, Other than the fact he would be driving a car.

"Let me tell you about my family. My full name is Christine Ann Taber Leonard. I was eighteen years old when you were born. Your father and I were not married, but we had the full support of our families. So when you were born, your father continued to get his education.

"He graduated from Harvard Business School top of his class. He works for the National Computer Technologies where his father is the CEO of the company. It is proving to be very successful. We have two children, Alyssa Marie Leonard who is sixteen and Trent Scott Leonard who is fourteen.

"We have traveled to this area many times and have stayed at the Strasburg Inn. We were only a short distance from our son all those times and never knew it. I remember one time when we were here just a year or so ago. We went to an Amish furniture store the Amish Cupboard. I purchased a chest there. I remember watching a young man working in the back of the shop. I was so taken with his skill and just could not move away from the window. Daniel, do you work at the Amish Cupboard, by any chance?" Christine asked.

"Yes I do, and I remember you because I was drawn to watching you too."

"We have lived very different lives. We have all the modern conveniences and advantages, and you have a simple life. Don't take that as a criticism of your lifestyle. I think we have too much sometimes. But when we were looking for you, I had the advantages of having the money I needed to look for you as well as the technology, cell phones, fax, and computers.

"I know that my parents as well as Ken's will be so happy to know that you have been found, and that you are a wonderful young man that has grown up in a loving family, and that you are doing well."

Amos spoke up, "We understand that you want your family to meet Daniel. If they would make the trip down, we would welcome them openly.

"Thank you. I know they would like that. I will call them tonight to see if they can all come. I know that Ken and the children will be down tomorrow."

The girls called into the front room to tell them that dessert was ready. They had put a pot of coffee on to perk and had sliced the pie. Amos spoke as they all settled at the table. "You all know that Daniel is not our natural child. He was adopted. This is our new friend and Daniel's mother."

The family all looked at Christine and smiled and welcomed her. Christine stayed for a while longer and then said good night. They talked about getting the whole family together for a meal, and that the Lapp family would be the guests of the Leonard's. Christine told Mary that she would talk to her when she had spoken to her family and they knew better when everyone would be there. "We will go to a nice place where we will be able to talk and get acquainted."

That night, back in her room, Christine called Ken. "Well, how did it go?" he asked as soon as he knew it was her.

"We have found our son. He does look just like the police photograph. He looks just like you did at age twenty. He has the heart-shaped birthmark just above his wrist, and his mother kept the clothes, blanket, and note that he came with."

"It is so hard to believe after all these years. I want to come down and meet him. I will be down there tomorrow. I'll bring Alyssa and Trent. We will need to tell our families, and maybe they will want to come down too. Oh, Jacob and Sally too. They could help with making Daniel comfortable with the rest of us. I am so excited. I know that I won't sleep tonight.

"I will call my parents and see if they can come and grandpa and grandma. I will call you back when I know how many will be coming so you can make reservations."

"Okay, I will call my parents too. I will talk to you later," Christine said, hanging up the phone.

Christine called her parents to tell them the news. They didn't even know that she was not in Owego. When she told them, they said that they too would be down tomorrow. Things were falling into place. When Ken called about forty-five minutes later, everyone was excited and looking forward to the trip and meeting Daniel.

Christine turned the TV on, but she was so excited that she wasn't watching it. She was thinking about everything that had happened in the last twenty-four hours. It was several hours that she was able to finally fall asleep.

The next morning she made reservations for everyone coming from New York and then went to Miller's Smorgasbord to make reservations for the next night. As Christine was making the arrangements, she realized that there would be a large group, twenty in all. She asked if they would have a private room for the group. They did and were able to put them in the only room that they had, which was much better for this diversified group.

As Christine was going back to the Inn, she thought about the photo album that they had from when Daniel was born. She called her mother to ask her to bring it. "It is funny that you called. I just picked it up and put it in the suitcase to bring."

"That is great. I am sure that Daniel would like to see the pictures of himself when he was born. When are you leaving to come down?" Christine asked.

"Well, your father is overseeing Chris right now. He is telling him that you have found Daniel. We'll finish up loose ends and leave first thing in the morning. So tell me about my grandson. Is he tall? Does he have dark hair?"

"He looks just like Ken did when he was twenty. He has light-brown hair and blue eyes, not too tall, maybe five foot ten inches. He is a handsome boy. He was very quiet, but that is to be expected. The Amish usually are very quiet around outsiders."

"Well, your father and I can't wait to meet him. We will be down sometime tomorrow afternoon. Did you make the reservations for us?"

"Yes. I guess I better get going. I want to do some shopping before Ken and the children get here. See you tomorrow. Love ya, Mom."

"Love you too. Bye."

CHAPTER 6

Daniel Meets the Family

Christine stopped by the Lapp home that afternoon to tell them that her family would be down the next day and that she had made reservations at Miller's for dinner tomorrow night. "I was able to get their private room. There will be twenty of us in all, and I thought it would be easier for all of us to have some privacy. I can make arrangements for a van to pick you up if you like."

"No, we will call our driver. We should have had your family here. I just never thought about it. Will your family still be here on Saturday?" Mary asked. "If they are, why don't we have a picnic. It would give our families a chance to fellowship in a casual environment."

"That sounds wonderful. Why don't you invite everyone tomorrow night?"

Christine said goodbye and headed to the outlet mall on Route 30. She shopped for several hours, buying an outfit for Alyssa, a video game for Trent, and a jacket for Ken. For herself, she bought a very simple dress to wear tomorrow to dinner.

After freshening up, Christine made her way to the dining room at the inn. She asked for a table near a window. From there, she could watch an Amish farmer and his sons working in the field. "It is hard to believe that my son is Amish. He has been brought up so differently than Alyssa and Trent." She would give Daniel the world if she thought he would accept it.

Once she was done with dinner, she decided to sit on the porch of the inn in one of the many rocking chairs. It was a wonderful area with it's neat Amish farms and patchwork lands. She felt such peace when she was here.

As she sat there thinking, something caught her attention: an Amish buggy coming down the road and pulling into the parking lot of the inn. It just looked so out of place there. As she watched, she saw a young Amish man emerge from the buggy and walk toward the inn. It took her a few minutes to realize that it was Daniel.

"Hello, Daniel."

"Hello, Mrs. Leonard. I came to visit you, just the two of us. Would that be all right?" he asked.

"That would be wonderful. I would like that very much. Have a seat."

They sat for a few minutes without speaking. Finally Daniel spoke. "I have always known that I was adopted, but I never thought that my parents were not Amish. I also always knew that I would meet them one day. Now that it is here, I'm nervous. I've met you, and I like you, and I feel comfortable with you. I just don't know how your children and your husband will accept me."

"Oh, Daniel, your father loves you. He has always loved you. When you went missing, we sat for hours and cried. We were up for hours, waiting to hear something about you. We lived on coffee and our love for each other and our love for you.

"Then your father had to leave to go back to college. He didn't want to go. He wanted to stay and wait for you to come home. But we finally convinced him to complete his education. It was important for him to be able to support us when you came home.

"But as we both know, that never happened. He mourned your loss as much as I did. I don't have any worries about your father. He loves you, and he will accept you just as you are. The important thing to him is that we finally found you.

"Now, as far as Alyssa and Trent, I don't know how they will relate to you. They have grown up totally opposite to the way you have. My gut feeling is that they will be shy at first, but they will be understanding. The important thing is that the relationship grow gradually as you all earn each other's trust and respect."

"Thank you. I don't want to do anything that will hurt my parents. They have given me a good life."

"We don't want to do anything to hurt your parents either. We do not want to take you away from your family. We just want the opportunity to get to know you and love you.

"Tomorrow, there will be a lot of people coming to dinner who love you and want to meet you. My mother-in-law's parents are coming too. They are the people I spoke of the other night, the ones that are former Amish. When you see them, you'll think they are still members of the Amish community. You may feel more comfortable with them than the rest of us.

"Your great-grandparents and are a lovely couple. Their names are Jacob and Sally King. Jacob is a woodworker just like you. You may have even inherited his skills."

"I look forward to meeting my new family. It is nice to know where I come from. Well, I guess I better get back home. I left after chores and before Bible reading. I will say goodbye for tonight, and we will see you tomorrow.

"Daniel, thank you for stopping by. We look forward to tomorrow night also."

Daniel got into his buggy and headed home. So much to think about. One thing for sure was that he really liked this woman who was his mother. It made him feel good to know that they had looked for him for so long.

He wondered why his uncle felt he needed to kidnap him and take him away. "Christine did say he had mental problems, so I guess that is why."

He wondered too what his grandparents and great-grandparents would think of him. She said that his great-grandparents were formerly Amish. Why did they leave the Amish fold? Where were they from? If they left the community, why did they continue to dress and stick to the Amish practices?

He had so many questions. He hoped that tomorrow night, his questions would be answered.

When Daniel arrived home, Bible reading was over, and most of the family had gone to bed. He found his parents in the kitchen having a cup of coffee and a piece of pie. "So you are home, son," Amos said.

"Would you like some coffee and cookies or a piece of pie?" his mother asked.

"Sure, that would be good. I went to see Christine. I had to make sure that everyone would be respectful to you tomorrow."

"Oh, Daniel, that was very sweet of you, but I don't think that Christine would let anyone do anything that would be disrespectful toward us. She is a good woman. She doesn't want anything to happen to this process of getting to know you after they have searched for so many years.

"It must have been terrible for them when you were kidnapped. I can't imagine what it would be like to have one of my children taken.

"Your father and I have been talking about having your new family over for a picnic on Saturday. We could do all the regular picnic food, play games, and maybe, just maybe, if everyone is interested, we could have a hayride. What do you think of that?"

"I think that would be very nice. It would be a more relaxed atmosphere, and playing games would be fun. I wonder if any of them have ever been on a hayride before? Could we build a bonfire and roast hot dogs after?"

"Well, yah. But if we roast hot dogs after the hayride, we need to do something different for the picnic," Mary said with her mind rushing forward.

"We could do barbecued chicken with potato salad, baked beans, coleslaw, bread, butter, and apple butter. Does that sound okay?" she asked.

"That would be good," Amos said. "At the weenie roast, we will need marshmallows, mustard, ketchup, rolls, and potato chips. That would be good. Hey, maybe I could make some homemade root beer. Would you like that?"

"Oh, Amos, that would be great."

When Daniel came down the next morning, he found his mother and sisters already in the kitchen baking pies. They were talking and laughing as they prepared the ingredients. Mary already had made some cinnamon rolls that were in the oven. They were pretty much a staple in the Lapp house; cinnamon rolls were everyone's favorite.

Daniel found his father and brothers in the barn. There was good-natured teasing going on, and they too were laughing and having a good time. This helped with getting the chores done, when everyone worked together and had a good time.

The family sat down to one of Mary's big breakfasts. This morning, she had made blueberry pancakes, bacon, ham, and scrambled eggs. Oh, and of course, cinnamon rolls. There was an air of happiness, and everyone was looking forward to dinner tonight and the picnic tomorrow.

"David, if you would hitch the horse to the buggy after breakfast, the girls and I must go buy supplies for the picnic. We need to get back to finish the baking, so we will leave as soon as breakfast dishes are cleaned up."

Breakfast done, the kitchen cleaned up, the girls loaded into the buggy and headed to Strasburg. Fridays and the weekend were busy in town because of the tourists. Once the shopping was done, they headed back home. They were all excited about the picnic. Mary was so pleased that the family was embracing Daniel's family and supporting him. They all loved him and wanted what was best for him.

The rest of the day passed quickly; and at 6:30 p.m., the Lapp family was ready and waiting for their driver. When they arrived at Miller's, the hostess escorted them into the private room where they were met by the smiling faces of Christine and her family. Christine made the introductions, of course, starting with Ken and Daniel. It was every emotional for Ken. "I am so glad to finally get to know you, Daniel. I hope that we'll become friends."

The last people that Christine introduced the Lapp family to were Elizabeth's parents, Jacob and Sally King. Just as Christine had said, they were dressed as if they were practicing Amish. Amos and Mary greeted the Kings and felt very comfortable with them. Everyone was very nice to them, and they did feel welcome. Also with the Lapp family were Amos's parents, Jonathan and Annie Lapp. They and the Kings got along very well for just meeting each other.

Daniel was curious about Alyssa and Trent. They were very nice to him and all his siblings. The young people wandered off to one side and were asking questions of each other. They were laughing and enjoying their small group. Daniel was quiet and just watched the interactions between his siblings—all of them, new and old.

The Tabers and the Leonards were enjoying watching their grandchildren. Who would have expected that Daniel was here in Lancaster County all these years. He was a fine young man. His adoptive parents were just the type of people they would have chosen to raise their grandson, if they had been given the choice.

After about fifteen minutes, the waitress came to start serving their meal. Everyone took their seats, and Ken stood and said a prayer. The meal was served, and everyone talked and ate and had a great time getting acquainted. What a wonderful evening. All the adults were enjoying each other's company. As they ate, one adult after another would make mention of how the young people were getting along.

As the evening was drawing to a close, Amos stood up and asked for everyone's attention. "The Lapp family would like to thank you for a wonderful evening. We would also like to invite you over to our farm for a picnic tomorrow afternoon and then a hayride and weenie roast in the evening."

Daniel watched the faces of the people in the room. Some had been on many hayrides and some had never been on one.

"That would be wonderful. What time would you like us to come, and what can we bring?" Christine asked.

"We will plan to eat around 5:00 p.m. There will be plenty of time for games following dinner before we go on the hayride," Amos said. "And you don't need to bring anything. Thank you."

"That sounds like so much fun. I have never been on a hayride," Alyssa said.

The Lapp young people couldn't believe that there was someone who had never been on a hayride. "You have a lot to look forward to," Daniel said. "Have you ever had a hot dog cooked on the end of a stick over an open fire?"

"No. I can hardly wait," Alyssa said.

"Tomorrow, Samuel and I will get the sticks prepared for our hot dogs. It is so much fun to cook them that way, and they taste so good."

"When we are at your house, will you tell us all about the farm? I am interested in everything," Alyssa told Daniel. "Remember that you are my big brother, and you need to teach me all about it."

Everyone laughed.

Shortly after that, they all said their goodbyes. Everyone was looking forward to the next day. As the Lapp family left in their van, Jacob said, "What a wonderful family they are. It is like I've known them all my life."

"I agree," Ken said.

Once the group from New York arrived at the inn, they decided to sit on the wonderful front porch and talk for a while. Alyssa and Trent went to their rooms to watch TV. "I, for one, really enjoyed getting to know them. Amos and Mary are fine people. It was nice to be with such good people and talk the language again," Jacob said.

"I was a little worried how it would go with the two cultures together, but I think it went well. They are wonderful people and a pleasure to be with. I really think I'm going to enjoy tomorrow. I haven't been on a hayride for a long time. It will be fun." Jacob went on to say.

"So, Ken, what do you think of your son?" his father asked.

"I am just in awe of this young man that is my son. He has been raised well and has an easy way about him. I wonder what the kids think of Daniel?

"Jacob, did you know that Daniel makes Amish furniture? When we were down here several years ago, I bought a small side table from the Amish Cupboard. When we were there, I was watching a young man in the back working on a piece of furniture. I could not take my eyes off him. Something about him drew me, and I didn't want to leave. When I spent the first evening with the Lapps, he told me he remembered me too. He said he was drawn to me. My son was right in front of me, and I didn't know it."

"You are certainly blessed to have found Daniel. Now he can get to know Alyssa and Trent. Even if he never comes to New York, we know where he is, and we can always come down to visit," Christine's father said.

"Is anyone interested in going to the Strasburg store for ice cream?" Dan asked.

"Sure, I will run up and get the kids," Ken said.

They all headed out for ice cream and a walk around town. It was a full day, and everyone had enjoyed it totally. Tomorrow would be as busy as today, so on returning to the inn, they all said good night and went to bed.

The next day dawned with much anticipation for the fun night ahead. After breakfast at the inn, the ladies decided to go to Bird-in-Hand to the market and to Intercourse to Zook's general store so Sally could buy some material. The men decided to go to the Strasburg railroad museum. Jacob had never been to the Lancaster area, so he wanted to see it all.

The ladies had lunch at the Family Cupboard Restaurant, and the men at the Strasburg Store and Creamery. At 5:45 p.m., the King, Leonard, and Taber families were getting into their cars to go to the Lapp farm.

At the Lapp farm, it has been a busy day too. The girls continued some baking, and Mary was preparing the potato salad and coleslaw for dinner. She also decided to make some Amish macaroni salad and deviled eggs. By the time the guests arrived, everything was ready, and Amos was outside standing at the grill cooking the chicken.

As Alyssa and Trent emerged from the car, Daniel and Samuel come up to show them the sticks for cooking the hot dogs.

Mary called, "Welcome, welcome," as she came out the back door. "We will be ready to eat in about fifteen minutes. Have a seat and relax. Did you have a good day?"

"We had a wonderful day. We went to the Bird-in-Hand market and then to Zook's so Sally would buy some material. Then we went to the Family Cupboard for lunch. The guys went to the railroad museum and then to the corner creamery for lunch."

Once the chicken was done, they all settled down for their meal. Same as the night before, the meal was filled with conversation and laughter. When the meal was over, Mary asked if anyone wanted dessert? In unison, "Oh, I can't eat another thing." was the response of the group.

"We'll have dessert at the campfire then."

"That sounds good."

The young people got up and headed to the field to play ball, and the men headed to the horseshoe pits. This was Amos's favorite pastime. He discovered that Jacob likes to toss horseshoes too.

As the women cleaned up after the meal, the conversation was light. The work was made easy with many hands. As the women entered Mary's kitchen, Sally stopped and looked around. It was like she was lost in time. "Is anything wrong Sally," Mary said.

"It is just that your kitchen is so like my mother's when I was growing up. I have wonderful memories of growing up Amish."

"Were you from the Lancaster area or someplace else?" Mary asked.

"When my ancestors came to this country, they settled in Ohio. My parents eventually moved from Ohio to a small community near Towanda, Pennsylvania, named Troy, Pennsylvania. My brothers and sisters still live there. I miss them, but we are shunned, so I haven't seen them in many years."

"Well, Sally, it is my understanding that you still live a simple life, and you obviously still dress Amish. I'm sure you could go back and ask for forgiveness."

"We could have years ago. But now Jacob, is so involved in the business that we couldn't just leave it. We don't have any sons to take over, and Elizabeth's husband is so busy, he couldn't possibly run our company along with the company he runs. So we live the simple life even though we are no longer Amish."

"Well, I don't know why you left the community, but it certainly is their loss."

Mary put a pot of coffee on to perk, and by the time it was ready, the cleanup work was done. They all settled down at the table to enjoy their coffee and some cookies. Mary asked Sally if she had ever done any quilting?

"I sure have. As a matter of fact, I am working on one now. I like quilting, but I was running out of people to give them to until I took one to the nursing home. They were so happy to get it that I take them there when I got one done. I keep them supplied with quilts for the patients, and it gives me something to do."

"What a wonderful gift to the patients. So often, the people in nursing homes are forgotten. A quilt is a bright and cheery addition to their life."

"Do you quilt, Mary?" Sally asked.

"I am just finishing one now. It is for Annie, for her wedding chest. As you know, Sally, but maybe the other ladies don't know, we start supplying the wedding chest from about the age of sixteen years of age on. Amos has also made her a chest to take to her new home."

"Is Annie to marry this fall?"

"We suspect that she will, but she hasn't said anything yet. The only thing she did say was maybe we should plant celery."

Outside, they could hear shouts and laughter. The ball game sounded like it was a great success. It was wonderful that the young people were getting along so well. They had really had a good time the night before, and now they were continuing where they left off.

It was about 8:00 p.m. when Amos got the horses and hitched them to the hay wagon and pulled it into the yard. "Come, everyone. It is time for the hayride," he called.

Mary had already placed several quilts in the wagon so people would either sit on them or cover up with them. Amos had put bales of hay around the sides of the wagon so they could either sit on them or lean up against them. Once everyone was seated, Amos started out of the yard. They had only gone about two hundred yards when Alyssa said, "This is so much fun. How come we have never done this before?"

The hayride lasted about an hour. By the time they returned to the house, everyone was ready for hot dogs. When Daniel got off the wagon, he went to start the fire, and Samuel went to get the sticks that they had prepared for everyone. The ladies went into the house to get the food for their roast.

The evening was perfect for a bonfire. There was just a little chill in the air, so you could be close to the fire to cook and not too hot.

"I don't know how to do this," Alyssa said. "I need help."

Daniel quickly went to her and showed her how to put the hot dog on the stick. "Now put it into the fire, but make sure you keep turning the stick so the hot dog doesn't burn."

Alyssa's first try was burned to a crisp. Everyone had a good laugh, but she tried again. Her second try turned out perfect. "We have to do this at home. Thanks, Daniel, for showing me what to do."

He responded with, "That's what a big brother is for."

After everyone had eaten their fill of hot dogs and desserts, the New Yorkers thanked the hosts and said their goodbyes. They would be leaving on Monday morning, but they would not see the Lapp family the next day because it was church day, and the family would be at church all day. Jacob explained on the way back to the inn that an Amish church service was three hours long, and then there was a community meal following the service. After the meal, the families stayed around and visited and played games.

When they arrived at the inn, everyone said their good night and headed for bed.

On Sunday, the northern group toured around the area. Amos and Sally enjoyed seeing the area. Every time they would see a mailbox with the King name on it, they would wonder if it might be family.

On their tour, they ate at a wonderful restaurant and stopped in Intercourse at the Kettle Kitchen where they bought James jelly, chowchow, and many other wonderful things. They enjoyed their day, and all spoke about returning soon.

That night they went to the dining room at the inn for dinner. Over the meal, they talked about everything that had taken place since Christine had received a call from Daniel. Trent had made friends with the Lapp children and took a fancy to Kate. As for Alyssa, she was quite attracted to David, and David really paid her quite a bit of attention.

Amos and Sally were so happy to be back in the company of members of the Amish community. They missed the fellowship of that close-knit order. They had really bonded with Amos and Mary, as had the rest of the group. They had also felt a closeness with Jonathan and Annie Lapp, Amos's mother and father. It was a comfortable, easy friendship, like they had always known each other.

Christine and Ken both felt a new peace after finding their son. They wanted Daniel to come to New York to see how they lived and where his roots were, but they wouldn't bring that up just now. They told Daniel that they would write to him and hoped he would write back.

Monday morning started out as a bright sunny day. The group from New York was packing their belongs and getting ready to head home. No one was in a hurry to leave. They had a leisurely breakfast and talked over coffee. Once back in their room, Ken discovered that there was a message at the desk for them. "I'll go down to see who it's from. Everyone is here that we would worry about."

At the desk, Ken found a message from Daniel. He called to tell them that his father became ill last night after they returned from their church service and was in the hospital. Amos was asking for Jacob to come to the hospital. Daniel asked that Ken bring Jacob to the Lancaster Medical Center.

Ken hurried upstairs to Jacob and Sally's room. Knocking at the door, he told them that he needed to speak to them. Jacob opened the door. "Come in, son."

"Grandfather, Amos Lapp is in the hospital and is asking for you. He got sick last night, and they took him to the medical center. I will take you."

Sally spoke up and said he must go, and she would go to be with Mary. Ken gathered everyone else in their room and told them about Amos and that he would be taking Jacob and Sally to the medical center. Christine spoke up and said, "I would like to go, but that would be too many people. I will go to the farm and see if there is anything I can do for them. Annie and Jonathan must be very worried."

Christine's father spoke up and said that they had to go home because he had an important meeting the next day.

"Maybe we should send Alyssa and Trent home with your parents," Ken said. "They can stay at your parents' house and go to school from there."

"We'll be okay with Mom and Dad? I'll go get the kids ready to go. What about your parents? Are they leaving?"

"Yes, my father has to fly to France tomorrow morning. They need to get home, so we can take grandpa and grandma home when they are ready to leave."

So Ken loaded up Jacob and Sally into his car and headed to the medical center.

James and Elizabeth and Carol Ann and Dan and the kids all left at the same time.

Once Christine had seen everyone on their way, she headed to the Lapp farm. When she arrived, she did not see anyone around the house, so she went the back door and knocked. Annie answered the door. "Christine, I didn't expect to see you today. I thought you were leaving for home. "Come in, come in."

"We were supposed to leave today, but we got a call from Daniel about Amos and him asking to see Jacob, so Ken took Jacob and Sally to the medical center, and the rest of the family all headed home. I decided to come here to see if there was anything I can do for you and your family."

"I was just about to put the tea kettle on. Would you like some tea?"

"I would love some. Where is everyone?"

"Jonathan and Daniel are at the medical center, and the rest of the family is at work. They decided to go to their jobs, but they will be home as soon as they are done for the day. I am here to stay by the phone."

"What happened to Amos? When we left on Saturday night, he seemed to be fine. By the way, we all had a wonderful time, and the kids haven't stopped talking about it."

"Oh, good. We had a great time too. It was after we came home from service yesterday that Amos started feeling bad. He started vomiting. And after several hours of that, he decided he needed to go to the hospital. So we called a driver, and they have been there since midnight."

"You haven't heard anything since then?"

"No, only that he had Daniel called Jacob and told him he wanted to see him. Do you know what that is about?"

The whistle on the kettle sounded off just then, and Annie got up to make the tea.

"I don't know. The only thing I do know is that they have become fast friends, and Jacob and Sally really like Amos and Mary."

Annie sat down and passed Christine her tea. The two women sat for some time just talking, getting to know each other better.

About an hour after Christine arrived, the phone in the shed started ringing. Annie hurried out to answer it. When she returned, she had a report from the hospital. Amos had an appendicitis attack, and he was in surgery to have it removed. She also said that Ken and Jacob were on their way to do the chores that needed to be done.

Christine laughed. "I have no doubt that Jacob can handle that, but Ken is another thing. I guess he will learn a little about the life our son lives, and that is a good thing."

"Well, if they are coming, I guess I better get some food out for them. My family will not be here for several hours yet. They will all be here for dinner."

The two women set about getting a noon meal ready. There were leftover salads from the picnic. The leftover chicken was quickly made into chicken salad. Everything was on the table as Ken pulled into the driveway. Samuel arrived home at the same time that Ken and Jacob arrived from the hospital. "How is Father? Have you heard anything?"

"Yes, he is in surgery to have his appendix removed. That is what was making him sick."

"Then he will be all right?" Samuel asked.

"Yes, but it will take him a long time to recover from it. We will have to work very hard to take over and do Father's chores. He does so much around here. I sure hope that everyone is willing to work to do the chores he does. It will be hard with all of us working in other jobs, not on the farm."

Jacob spoke up then, "Your father has asked me if I would be willing to stay and help until he is back on his feet again, and Sally and I have consented. We will live in the Dawdi house until Amos is ready to take over again."

Once Ken and Jacob had filled everyone in on what had gone on at the hospital, they all sat down to eat. Samuel was the first to speak after they started to eat. "I just can't help staring at Jacob. He looks so much like father. I noticed it first at Miller's and then again the night of the picnic and hayride. You look enough alike to be brothers.

Annie looked at Jacob with a strange look on her face. "Yeah, you're right. Maybe they are related, and we don't know it." But Annie started thinking. What if this was her son. He was from Troy, and that is where Kate and Samuel settled when they left Strasburg. It couldn't possibly have happened that way, could it? For her long-lost son to reappear in her life when she thought she had lost him forever?

When Samuel said something again about their being related, Anne said, "I don't think they are. Jacob is from Troy, and your father has always lived in Strasburg."

"I don't think so either. I have a twin sister Rebecca Ruth and three brothers. My family moved from Lancaster when I was very young. I asked once if we could come back to visit, but it was not possible. It was almost like my father was afraid to come back. Maybe somehow we are related, but I guess we will never know. Now I must get to the chores. Coming, Ken?" Jacob asked.

Ken, Jacob, and Samuel headed out the door. "I am happy to help Amos in this way. I know that Jonathan has his own chores to do, and you boys are good, but you can't do everything and work too. Before we know, it Amos will be fit as a fiddle and ready to get back to work."

As the men headed to the barn, the women cleaned up the kitchen and talked about making chicken and noodles for dinner. They quickly prepared four chickens for the oven and got them cooking. "When the chicken is done and cool, we will be able to take it off the bone. The drippings we'll put in a pot with chicken broth and some carrots and celery. Let that cook and add the noodles and chicken. And once the noodles are cooked, we're ready to eat."

"Sounds wonderful," Christine said.

"We will plan on everyone for dinner tonight. Daniel said he and his mom will leave the hospital after Amos is out of surgery. He will need to rest, and so will Mary. She has been up all night and I am sure has been very worried about Amos. After Jacob and Ken have completed the chores with the boys, they'll be ready for a good meal," Annie said with a smile.

But Christine had noticed a change in Annie ever since lunch today. Something was bothering her, and it wasn't that she was worried about Amos. "Tell me about Amos's family. Does he have brothers and sisters?"

"Well, let's see. Amos has three brothers and two sisters. Jonathan and I met when we were working in Hummelstown. We got married and had our family there before we decided to return to the Strasburg area. We have a wonderful life here. My family home is only a mile from here to the west, and Jonathan's family is a mile to the east.

"Years ago, Amos was gifted my parents' house. He worked the farm for a while, and his grandparents lived in the Dawdi house that is attached to the main house until they died. My parents still live there but are very elderly and don't get out at all anymore."

"Annie, what is a Dawdi house?" Christine asked.

"A Dawdi house is a house that is added to the main house for our parents to live in when they get too old to take care of themselves and need help. It is a very nice thing to have three generations in the same house. Would you like to see this Dawdi house?" she asked Christine.

Annie led the way into the addition known as the Dawdi house. They walked all through. Christine was just so taken aback by it. "This is charming."

When they had returned to the main house, Christine asked Annie if she had a large family?

"Yes! I have eight brothers and sisters. They all live in this area but one. She and her husband moved to Troy, Pennsylvania many years ago. I think that is near you, isn't it?"

CHAPTER 7

Annie's Story

On November 3, Annie King was born into a family that already had four children. Samuel and Mary already had three girls and a boy; now there was another daughter. She was a pretty baby with blonde hair, blue eyes, and dimples when she smiled.

As Annie grew, so did the family. By the time Annie was ten years old, there were four more boys in the family. Annie's siblings were Kate, Susan, Sally, Joseph, Jacob, Daniel, John, and Jonah—all healthy, active children.

Annie attended school with other Amish children in a one-room schoolhouse where she first met Jacob Deitweller. He was the love of her life, and she was the love of his life. Jacob was a year older than Annie and had always looked out for her. When the young people had singings, he was always the center of attention, and every girl hoped that she would be the one he would ask to ride home in his buggy, but he only had eyes for Annie.

It was late August, just before school started, when Jacob asked her to ride home with him. She almost fell off the bale of hay, but of course she said yes. The rest of the night was spent waiting for the singing to be over.

The first time she rode home with Jacob, she was really shy. He was so handsome, and all the girls wanted to be Annie. They had a wonderful drive home. It was a nice warm night, and the stars were all shining brightly. As they road along, their conversation was light and filled with laughter. When they drew near the King home, Jacob said, "I am so glad you let me bring you home. I really like you,

Annie. You're different from the other silly girls. You have a good head on your shoulders."

"Thank you, Jacob. I have had a good time riding with you. I like you too. I like it that you don't act stupid like some of the other boys."

"How about letting me take you home again in two weeks?" Jacob asked.

"I would like that."

As they pulled into the drive, Jacob reached over and took her hand and gave it a squeeze.

"Thank you, Jacob," Annie said as he hopped out of the buggy.

"Thank you, Annie, and I can't wait until we can do this again. Good night."

"Good night."

Annie could hardly sleep that night. She tossed and turned as she thought about Jacob. She was so fidgety that her older sister Kate asked her what was wrong. Kate and Annie were very close, and Kate had always taken an interest in all Annie did. "I'm just so happy." Annie said.

"Did something happen to make you so happy?"

"Yes. Don't tell, but someone brought me home in his buggy."

"Do you want to tell me who, or just keep it to yourself?"

"I'll tell you. It was Jacob Deitweller."

"Oh, he is a nice boy. His parents and his brothers and sisters are nice too. I have gotten to know his sister Katie, and we have such a good time together. That's great, Annie. Now *go to sleep.*"

Annie fell asleep with a smile on her face and hope in her heart.

Two weeks later, she rode home with Jacob again. This time, he took the long way to her house. They laughed and talked and had a wonderful time.

And so it went. Annie was done with school in June, and she could get a job. She was hoping to find one soon so she could start saving her money.

Jacob had been out of school for a year by then and had found a job in a woodshop in Strasburg. He was very talented and enjoyed being able to create things out of wood. He too was saving his money and was happy that by next June, he could ask Annie to be his bride.

She found a job in a store in downtown Strasburg that was only a block from where Jacob worked. They were able to see each other several times a week and often had lunch together. When Annie and Jacob weren't at work, they were helping their families. All hands were needed to run a busy farm, and they did what they could to help out.

Their lives went on this way; only now, they were seeing each other more often than ever. They would go and get ice cream or just take a leisurely drive in Jacob's buggy. Finally, in September, Jacob asked if he could take her to dinner on Saturday night. "I would like that," she replied

"I'll pick you up at 6:00 p.m., and we will go to the restaurant in town."

Sure enough, at 6:00 p.m., Jacob pulled into the drive. Greeting everyone, he said it was good to see them all. Annie was ready, and they left for Strasburg shortly after that. The restaurant wasn't fancy, but the food was wonderful.

"Annie, I think you know by now how I feel about you. I have wanted to ask you this before now, but I also needed to work and save money. Annie, I want you to be my bride. I have loved you from the first day you walked into the schoolhouse. Will you marry me in November?"

"Oh, Jacob. Yes, I will marry you. I wouldn't marry anyone else."

Once they had completed their meal, they left the restaurant and drove around the countryside for a long time. "I guess I better take you home. It is getting late. But soon, I won't be taking you home to your parents. I'll be taking you home to our house."

"Won't that be wonderful?"

After Jacob dropped Annie off at home, he drove home at a leisurely pace, thinking about the surprise he had for Annie. All these months he had been working on something for her, and he had a lot of help. He was building her a house with the help of family and friends. He and his father had drawn up the plans together. It was just a perfect size for a newlywed couple and even had a few extra bedrooms that when the children came along, they could continue living in the house for some time.

On the ground level, there was a big kitchen with a big pantry, a large front room with a big fireplace, a sewing room, and a half bath. On the second level, there were four bedrooms and a full bath. Just off the back porch, there was a room for the freezer and the laundry room. In the basement, there was all kinds of storage for canned goods. The house was located just east of Jacob's parents' house. There was a path through a wooded area to the house. It would take just a minute or two to walk from one house to the other.

His father, brothers, and brothers-in-law had all been working on the house with him. His family knew that he had someone special, although they weren't exactly sure who it was. The outside of the house was fieldstone. Jacob and his brothers had spent many hours picking stone from the fields and put them aside for the house. It was a beautiful house, and his mother had fallen in love with it. She had even told him that if his family got too big for the house, she and his father would trade with them.

Now that the house was done, they needed furniture. So Jacob spent every evening working on the furniture that they would need for their new house.

The night that Jacob asked Annie to marry him, she found her sister waiting for her. "How was your evening?' she asked Annie

"It was very nice, very nice. How was yours?"

"Annie, I have to tell you, but you must keep it a secret. I'm getting married."

Annie was surprised and asked, "Who is it that has won your heart?"

"Samuel Deitweller"

"Oh, Kate, that is wonderful. I also have a secret, and you must not tell either. I'm getting married too."

"Do I know who you are marrying?" Kate asked.

"I am marrying Jacob Deitweller, as if you didn't know."

The girls both laughed about their marrying brothers.

"Do you and Jacob have a date in mind?" Kate asked.

"Yes, he mentioned November. What about you?"

"I think it will be the first part of December for us. We need to find a place to live."

"Us too. I wonder if Jacob has given that any thought?"

November came and the first wedding of the community was Jacob and Annie's. There would be about four hundred people at their wedding, and to think that Annie's parents would be doing it again in just a month was almost more than most people could think about. There was much to do before the wedding. It is typical that the bride would not only make her dress, but the dresses of her attendants' which is Pennsylvania Dutch for side sitters.

Most brides pick blue as the color of their wedding dress, but Annie—being Annie—would be different. She chose a dark plumb for her dress; and for her newhochers, she chose light-lavender. Her sister Kate did pick blue for her and her attendants. It was a busy household with two brides preparing for their weddings. When Annie wasn't using the sewing machine, Kate was.

Celery, which is a tradition at an Amish wedding, was planted—a double batch. Amish weddings are usually on a Tuesday or a Thursday so that they have time to clean up before the next church service.

The preparations for the wedding started weeks before the event with women from their church coming to the bride's home to help clean the house from top to bottom. Then, they come and help bake and prepare foods, and some take chickens home the day before the wedding to roast and bring back for the wedding feast. When you are feeding four hundred, people it takes a lot of food. So the day before Annie's wedding there was a flurry of activity around the King house. The house was ready for the wedding. There were several women there helping with more cooking and baking, and the men and boys were making sure that the yard and grounds were ready to park all the buggies that would be there. They also had several farm wagons going to pick up benches for the congregation to sit on.

Following the wedding, there would be a feast with all the food prepared by family and friends. The menu is always the same: roast chicken, mashed potatoes, gravy, creamed celery, apple sauce, coleslaw, cherry pie, fruit salad, bread, butter, jelly, donuts, tapioca pudding, and usually a wedding cake. That is what would be served at Annie and Jacob's wedding. There is also another meal at the dinner hour, and that menu differs from the wedding feast menu; but again, the food is prepared by family and friends.

Finally, the day of Annie and Jacob's wedding arrived, and it arrived early. Since the wedding service starts at 8:30 a.m., the family has to be up early so they can have their chores done before people start to arrive. So everyone was up at 4:00 a.m. The helpers start to arrive at 6:30 a.m.; and by 7:30, the bride and her attendants are waiting to greet the guests for the wedding. When the guests arrive, they are greeted, and then the Forgehr—ushers, married couples—take them to their seats.

Finally. At 8:30 a.m., the service begins. While the congregation sings some hymns, Annie and Jacob were counseled by the minister in another part of the house. When they return to the congregation, the service begins with a prayer, scripture reading, and a sermon. Then the minister calls Annie and Jacob forward. He asked them some questions and then blesses the couple, and they return to their seats. A prayer is spoken, and the service is over.

Once the service had ended, the women started getting the food to the tables for the wedding feast. It takes a long time to serve everyone. Once they had eaten, the guests visit in small groups around the house, and the children play games. At 5:00 p.m., the feeding starts again. This time, the bride and groom's parents are in the first group to eat. And finally, at around 10:30 p.m., the bride and groom say good night to the last of their guests.

They all hurried off to bed because the King family knew that the next day would be almost as busy as today was. Annie and Jacob stayed at the King's home that night so they would be there first thing in the morning for cleanup.

Jacob hadn't shown or told Annie about the house he had built. She thought they were going to live in the Dawdi house on the Deitweller farm. Once the house was cleaned and everything was back in order at the King's, Annie and Jacob said goodbye and headed to the Deitweller farm and their cozy little Dawdi house, or so Annie thought.

As Annie and Jacob pulled into the drive at the Deitweller's, Jacob said, "What's that?" pointing to the right of the house at a light in the woods. "Let's go see"—he guided to the house in that direction.

"Jacob, there is a house there," Annie said. "Who put a house there?"

By now, they were pulled up in front of the beautiful two-story stone house. Jumping out of the buggy, Jacob said, "Come on."

"Do you think we should? Who lives here?" she asked

As they stepped on the porch, Jacob said, "You do." And with that, he picked her up and carried her into the house. Stopping inside, he kissed her and put her down. There was a nice fire in the fireplace, so the room was nice and warm.

"What do you mean? This is our house?"

"Yes, I built it for us. My dad and I made the plans. And with the help of a lot of people to build it, we got it done for us to live in. Happy wedding."

Annie didn't know what to say. She didn't know whether to laugh or cry or both. It was completely furnished and just perfect. She walked around looking at everything. "Where did the furniture come from?" she asked.

"Well, I made that too. Again, I had help from my family, your family, and our friends. Do you like it?" Jacob asked.

"I love it. It is more than I could ever dream of. I love you, Jacob Deitweller."

"And I love you, Annie Deitweller.

After looking around the house for many more minutes, they went to bed and spent their first night in their new home.

Every day was a joy. Jacob and Annie worked hard and played hard, but every night would find them in their cozy home. Their lives were full of love and happiness.

In just a few short weeks following their wedding, it was time for Kate and Samuel's wedding. Again, the King house was a flurry of activity. The wedding was a love-filled ceremony, and everyone enjoyed themselves. Kate and Samuel settled in the Dawdie house on the Deitweller farm. The Dawdi house was built on the main house for Samuel's grandparents when they were alive. Since they had passed away, it was the perfect place for Samuel and Kate to live since Samuel was working on the farm with his father.

The winter months passed; and by spring, Annie was pregnant with their first child. Jacob was overjoyed. It was something that they had hoped for, and now they would have a wee one. "I will make a cradle that will go in our room for when the baby first comes home. Close to Mommy and Daddy," Jacob said.

When they told Annie's parents, they were so happy for the young couple. For Jacob's parents, it was their first grandchild, and they could hardly wait. It was only a week later that Kate and Samuel made an announcement that they too were expecting. What an exciting time for the two couples.

It was a busy summer: the farming and planting, planting the house gardens, and preparations for two new babies, as well as all the social activities that go on in the summer months.

Jacob and Annie talked one night about the cradle he was making for their child. "Oh, I should make one for Kate and Samuel," Jacob said. "I will really have to work hard to get them both done in time."

When Jacob wasn't working in the shop in town or helping on the farm, he could be found in his workshop making not one, but two cradles.

Everything in the life of the newlyweds was going great. Annie was adjusting to being a new wife and soon to be a mother. As harvest time approached, Annie and Kate were busy making baby clothes and baby blankets. Annie often thought what a joy it was to be sharing this experience with her beloved sister.

Thanksgiving was a busy time for both the young couples. The first part of the day was spent at the Deitweller farm with all the family and the traditional Thanksgiving feast. By midday, the two couples were at the King farm for yet more food. "I have eaten so much today that I can hardly move," Annie said after the meal at her parents. She was beaming; being pregnant agreed with her. Kate too was doing great, but she just did not have the energy that Annie had.

There was, after all, four years difference in their ages, and it would be harder on Kate.

December started with a snowstorm that dumped several inches of snow on the Lancaster Valley. That was unusual for that early in the season, and Jacob was concerned. What if Annie decided to have the baby early? How would he get her to the hospital? Not to worry because a few days later, the snow had all melted.

Annie went into labor while Jacob was at work. She went to the main house, and her mother-in-law called Jacob from the phone shed to tell him, "I will call a driver, and we will stop and pick you up on our way. Now don't worry. This is a very normal and natural process. We will be there soon."

When she got off the phone, she went to get Annie's things from the house. Stopping at the barn, she told her husband it was time for Annie to be delivered. She was just returning to the house when the van pulled into the drive. Annie and her in-laws got in and took off, leaving Kate waving goodbye as they pulled away.

After picking up Jacob, they arrived at Lancaster General at about 11:00 a.m. on February 12. Annie was in hard labor, and by 4:00 p.m., she and Jacob were the proud parents of a fine son named Jacob King Deitweller. The doctor said he was healthy, and Annie had done well. Jacob was allowed to see Annie, who was quite tired; and once he was sure she and his son were doing fine, he made his first call to his brother Samuel to let him know about the baby. Nobody answered the phone, but that wasn't unusual. He left a message with all the information about the baby, and all they would want to know. Then he called the King house to let them know about their new grandson.

While Annie was resting, Jacob had time to reflect on the day. It was a time to think he was so blessed. He had a wonderful wife and now a son. They lived in a house that he had built for them, and their life was filled with joy. "He truly is the most beautiful baby," Jacob said to his parents.

Putting her hand on his, his mother agreed with him.

A short time later, Annie was awake and ready for company. Jacob and his parents went to her room. While they were talking, the doctor came in to check her out. "I just checked your son out, and he is fine. If everything stays as it is now, you will be able to take him and his mother home tomorrow."

"That would be wonderful. Thank you, Dr. Hill."

"I will have everything ready for you when we get you home," Jacob said to Annie.

They sat there talking for a long time. Jacob's parents talked about the day he was born. "Jacob was born at home, not in a fancy hospital. Back then, unless there was a problem, most Amish babies were born at home."

Out in the hall, there was some kind of disturbance. There were people hollering instructions to each other, and people were running up and down the hall. "There must be some kind of an emergency," Jacob said.

Jacob finally got up to look out in the hall. When he did, he saw an Amish man standing at the nurse's station. He had his back to Jacob, so he could not see his face. Jacob looked down the hall in the opposite direction but did not see anything. Looking back at the man standing at the counter, he realized that it was Samuel. He quickly hurried over to him. "Samuel, what is going on? Is something wrong?" he asked.

"After Mom and Dad left with Annie, Kate started having pains in her back, so she went to lie down. They got worse, and by the time I came to check on her, she was in hard labor. I called the ambulance, and before they could get there, she had the baby. When the attendants arrived, they quickly took Annie and the baby out and told me I could not ride in the ambulance and would need to find another ride to the hospital. So here I am. I don't know what is going on. I don't know if Kate is okay, and I don't know about the baby."

"Samuel, let me get Mom and Dad."

"Mom, Dad, come quickly. Samuel is here. Kate had the baby at home after you left, and the ambulance has rushed her and the baby here to the hospital, and Samuel does not know what is happening."

"Is Kate all right?" Annie wanted to know.

"I know that Kate is a strong girl, and I am sure that she is fine. They just have to check everything out to make sure that she and the baby are all right." Jacob told her.

It was about a half an hour later when Samuel came into Annie's room with his parents.

"Is everything okay?" Annie asked.

"Everything is fine. They told me that they just have to be very careful when there is a birth like that and wanted to make sure that Kate and the baby were both okay."

"Well, what is it? A boy or a girl?" Annie asked.

"It's a girl. I have a daughter."

A short time later Kate was wheeled into the room. "Do you mind that I share a room with you?" she asked. "I also did not mean to steel your thunder, but I just couldn't help it."

"I am happy that it is you that I am sharing the room with, and I know that our children will grow up very close, having the same birthday. What is her name?"

"Her name is Rebecca Ruth Deitweller," Kate said.

There was more discussion, but Kate was looking very tired.

Samuel's mother finally said, "I think we should leave and let Kate get some rest. I am sure that the Kings will be here tonight to see their new grandchildren."

"Oh no!" Samuel said, "I forgot to call your parents."

"What did you forget to call her parents about?" Mary asked as she and Samuel entered the room.

As Mary looked at the room, she saw Annie in the first bed, and then she saw Kate in the second bed. "What is going on?"

"Mama, I had my baby at the house after the family left with Annie. Samuel was in the field and came in to find me in hard labor. He called the ambulance, but before the ambulance arrived, Samuel had to deliver the baby. He was wonderful. I am so proud to have a husband that was able to do that."

"Is the baby all right?" Samuel, Kate's father, asked.

"She is fine. You have a granddaughter. Rebecca Ruth Deitweller."

"We must go to the nursery and see the babies. We didn't stop on our way in. If we had, we would have gotten a shock, I think. We would have thought that Annie had twins."

When they returned to the room after seeing the babies, they stayed around for only a short time to visit. When the Deitwellers decided it was time for them to leave, the Kings decided to leave too.

"We can share a van, if that is okay with you," Samuel said.

On the drive home, Jacob told the Kings that Annie would be coming home the next day. "I have a lot to do tonight to get the house ready for the new baby," he said.

"I will come over in the morning and help you get it ready."

"I will come too and help. That way, you can just concentrate on getting Annie and Jacob and bringing them home."

"When is Kate coming home, Samuel?" Mary asked.

"The doctor said she may be able to come home tomorrow too."

"It looks like we could have a busy day tomorrow, doesn't it?" Sally said to Mary.

As everyone thought, Annie and Kate were both released the next day. Sally had gotten up early and worked on making sure the Dawdi house was ready for the new baby and preparing some meals for the young couple. Mary had come over to Jacob's and helped make sure everything was ready for Annie and the baby to come home. She had brought a casserole to put in the oven for their dinner that night.

Life changed for the two couples, and they grew and flourished. Both Jacob and Rebecca were growing faster than anyone wanted them to. They were good and easily adjusted to changes in their routine. Kate and Annie grew even closer than they had been before. They were constantly exchanging ideas and tips.

By the time summer arrived, the babies spent much of their time outside in the yard on a blanket in the warm sun. While they played on the blanket, Annie and Kate worked in the garden, weeding and harvesting the vegetables that were ready to use.

It was late August when the fields were being harvested, and everyone was busy. Jacob was helping his father and brother stack hay in the barn. His father had gone to get the next wagonload of hay to be unloaded when Samuel descended the ladder to direct his father into the barn.

As he as stepping off the ladder, one of the barn cats ran under his foot, and he lost his balance. As he was trying to regain his balance, he kicked a lantern. The lantern was lit. Instantly, the barn caught fire, and with the hay on the floor, the fire spread fast, so fast that Jacob became trapped in the hay loft. There was no other way for him to get down.

Samuel ran from the barn, letting everyone know that the barn was on fire. As he was running across the yard to the phone shed, he hollered to his father that the barn was on fire. John came running and tried to control the fire with buckets of water, but it was no use. After Samuel called the fire department, he and his father continued to try to put the fire out.

With all the noise, Kate, Annie, and Sally came running from the house. "Where is Jacob?" Annie asked as she stood watching the fire burn.

John looked at Samuel, "Where *is* Jacob?" When Samuel didn't respond, John asked again, grabbing Samuel by the shoulders, "Son, where is Jacob?"

Samuel looked at his father and pointed to the barn.

"What are you saying? Is he still in the barn? In the loft?"

"He is trapped in the hay loft. The ladder burned, and he is trapped in the loft," Samuel said as his voice cracked with emotion.

Upon hearing that, Annie started running to the barn, but John caught her by the arm. "You can't go in there. I hear the fire trucks coming now. They will get him out."

Annie kept screaming Jacob's name, but she never got a response.

As the fire trucks pulled into the drive, Annie went running to the truck, telling them that her husband is trapped in the hay loft. The firefighters quickly ran to the barn with a ladder, but as they tried to enter the loft, they found that the fire had totally engulfed the entire area.

It took the fire department some time to get the fire under control. All the time, Annie sat on the grass and watched. Kate tried to get her to go into the house, but she just sat there and stared at what was once the Deitweller barn. The fire was out, the barn was destroyed, and Jacob was dead. What would she do without Jacob? How could her life go on?

"Annie, you need to come and sit in the house. I will fix you something to eat," Kate said.

"I don't want anything to eat. I don't need anything to eat," Annie said as she walked away. She walked to the house that she and Jacob had shared, the house that he had spent many hours building for her, for them and their family.

Sally walked with her. Annie did not respond to any of Sally's questions; she just walked looking straight ahead. "What about the baby, Annie? Do you want us to keep him tonight?"

"You keep him tonight and every night. I can't have him if I don't have Jacob." She entered their house and told Sally that she needed to be alone; and with that, she closed the door and locked it.

Sally walked back to her house. She was feeling such deep sorrow, but Annie needed her help. For now, she would take care of Jacob and wait for Annie to come around after such a shock.

As she walked into the yard, there were several Amish buggies pulling into the drive, and there were several already there surveying the damage. Word travels fast in the Amish community. Even without phones, it is amazing how quickly people know about tragedies in the midst of their quiet lives.

Many of the brethren had questions about the fire. How did it start? Where was Jacob that he couldn't get out? They asked John and tried to talk to Samuel, but he was in such a shock that he could not respond to the questions. He blamed himself for the fire. If he hadn't been so clumsy and lost his balance, Jacob would be alive right now.

Seeing that Samuel was in such distress, the bishop pulled him aside and tried to talk to him. "Samuel, God has a plan for us even before we are born. He knows exactly when our work here is done, and Jacob's work was done. He called him home, and you will see him again when you are also called home."

But Samuel was just not listening. It was his fault, and that was all there was to it.

Kate and Annie's parents had heard about the fire; and soon, they too were pulling into the drive. By the time they got to the

Deitweller farm, the fire was out, the fire company had left, and the bishop had already talked to Samuel. Sally told Mary that Annie was in a bad way. "She has locked herself in their house. She doesn't even want the baby. I don't know what we're going to do."

Mary told everyone that she would go and try to talk to her. When she arrived at Annie's house, Annie would not answer the door. She could see her sitting in the rocking chair—the rocking chair that Jacob had made for her—staring at the wall. Mary offered up a prayer. "Lord, please help us. How can I reach my daughter in the state that she is in."

Mary slowly made her way back to the Deitweller house. As she entered the yard, a group of men, including the bishop and the deacons, were gathered around Samuel. She went to talk to Kate and Sally. "Would she let you in?" Sally asked.

"No. She is sitting in her rocking chair just staring at the wall. I don't know what to do for her."

"Maybe we just need to give her time. She has had a terrible shock."

By the time Mary and Samuel left for home, several more buggies had arrived. The police had arrived to do an investigation of the fire and the death; but as they could see, it was just an accident, but they would do a complete investigation and then close the case.

Three days later was Jacob's funeral. He was placed in a plain wooden box with six sides. Usually, there is a split lid, but the lid could not be opened because of the condition of Jacob's body. The funeral lasted for two hours. At an Amish funeral, there is no eulogy, songs, or flowers. Once the funeral at the home was over, the body is taken to the cemetery for burial. Jacob's grave had been hand dug, and there was just a simple marker to mark the grave.

Annie did attend, but she spoke to no one. She kept her eyes on the box that held her husband, the love of her life. Kate and Samuel had taken over with little Jacob because Annie was still refusing to care for him. Her grief was so deep, she couldn't think about anything but Jacob.

As the box was lowered into the grave, Annie cried. Slowly, she turned to Samuel and started yelling at him. "You killed my husband! It is your fault. How can you live with yourself?"

Quickly, her parents drew her away. Getting her settled in the buggy, her father spoke softly to her. "Annie, it was an accident. Samuel would never hurt his brother. You need to pray about this. The Lord will help you."

"You pray to your Lord. My Lord deserted me. Take me home."

When they got to Annie's house, they asked her if she wanted them to stay. "No," and with that, she jumped out of the buggy and ran to the house and locked the door.

As her parents pulled out of the yard, her father said, "This is a concern. She needs help."

The next day, Annie's father went to talk to the bishop and deacons. It was decided that they would pay her a visit the next morning. When they arrived, they knocked on the door but did not get an answer. They tried several times, but still no response. Samuel tried the door; it was unlocked, so they entered the house. They called her name, but she did not respond. Samuel quickly searched the house; she was not there. But when they looked in the kitchen, Samuel found a note on the table. He picked it up and read it. As he read, the men saw the concern on his face. "What is it, Samuel?"

"I will read it to you."

> I have gone away. I cannot go on without Jacob, and I cannot stay where the person responsible for his death is still able to walk around as if nothing has happened. I can't stand to be around him. Samuel Deitweller killed my husband. And when he killed Jacob, he killed me too. Since he has taken Jacob, he may as well have his son too. Goodbye. Annie.

"This is terrible. What are we going to do? We don't know when she left. She could have been gone for forty-eight hours or more, and she could be a long way away by now."

They went to the Deitweller house to ask if anyone had seen her leave. They were shocked but said they did not see her leave. Kate and Samuel had seen the men and came to the main house.

The bishop had already shown the note to John and Sally; and when Samuel arrived, they showed it to him.

"I did not mean for it to happen. I lost my balance and bumped the lantern," Samuel said with such terrible pain in his eyes.

"Samuel, we know that it was an accident. In time, Annie will realize it too."

That day and that note changed the lives of Kate and Samuel Deitweller forever. The Amish brethren knew that the accident was taking a terrible toll on Samuel. He blamed himself for the fire and now the disappearance of Annie. He got very quiet, wouldn't eat, and just sat in his chair with his Bible on his lap. When the family could convince him to go to service, someone would say something about the fire, and that would send him even deeper into depression. Samuel couldn't bring himself out of it. Jacob was dead, Annie has gone who knows where, and little Jacob was without his parents, and that was his fault.

One morning, John said to him, "I would like to take you to talk to someone who may be able to help you with your thoughts of guilt."

Samuel said, "No."

Every few days, John would say this to Samuel until one day, he finally said he would go. John took him to Deacon Beiler, an old but very wise man. He had known Samuel and Jacob all their lives. When they arrived at the deacon's farm, they found him in the kitchen, reading *The Budget* and drinking coffee. "Come in, Samuel. Come in, John," he said as he opened the door. "Would you like some coffee and a sweet roll? My bride made them this morning."

"We would love some," John said, speaking for both of them.

Once they were settled at the table with their coffee and sweet rolls, the deacon started to talk to Samuel. "Samuel, I know how you feel."

"No, you don't. Nobody does."

"Oh, but that is where you are wrong. I had the same thing happen to me. I mean the very same thing. I bumped a lantern in the barn, it started a fire, and my brother was trapped in the hayloft. He died in that fire, just like Jacob died in the fire at your farm. It was an accident, and so was your fire. My brother was younger than Jacob, though."

"Annie hates me so. She has left her child and her family because she can't stand to be around me."

"Samuel, Annie is hurting, just like you are hurting. She is unable to handle this loss, and she is lashing out at you. It is not right that she has left, but I feel she will be back soon. The Lord will tell her that Jacob is fine, and that she needs to come home for her son's sake."

Samuel and John stayed for a short time longer, then went home. As they pulled into the drive, Samuel's eyes automatically went to the burnt remains of the barn, the constant reminder of what happened. In a few more days, there would be a barn raising, and the reminder of the place where Jacob died will be gone forever—gone forever from view, but never out of Samuel's mind.

"I have a headache. I need to lie down," Samuel said as he got out of the buggy.

Entering the Dawdi house, Kate saw he was upset. "How was your talk with Deacon Beiler?" she asked.

"Did you know that he once bumped a lantern and started a fire that killed his brother?"

"No, I didn't."

"Well, he thinks that because the same thing happened to both of us, it is something to just get over. I can't. I can't stand being here," he said as he looked around the house. "I can't stand being on this farm. I can't deal with Jacob's death. Every day, I walk out that door, and there in front of me is the burned out barn. I can't stand myself. I need to leave this place."

"No, Samuel, I need you here. I will go with you wherever you think you need to go. But we, Rebecca Ruth and I, and of course little Jacob, will go with you, and we will start a new life together."

They talked for a long time, and Samuel said he would not leave without all of them.

A few days later, Samuel sat down in his chair near the fireplace to read his copy of *The Budget*, the Amish newspaper. He had been rereading for several minutes when he came across an article about a small community of Amish near the town of Troy, Pennsylvania, which is north of Harrisburg. He read the article and liked what he read. There was plenty of property there that could be purchased and no one knew them there. There wouldn't be any questions about the fire.

Over the next few weeks, he made inquiries about Troy and found out as much as he could. Kate could see that Samuel had changed, but he was not back to the way he was before. She had read the article too, and they talked about relocating there. "I know you will miss your family, but we will make new friends," Samuel said.

"Yes, we will," Kate replied.

They didn't discuss their plans with anyone. They decided to wait until all the arrangements were made before saying anything. Samuel got the address of a family in Troy and had written to them, asking questions about the availability of property in the area. The reply that came back was all positive. Benjamin Esh said that the farmhouse and property next to him was for sale, and that it was a fine piece of land with a big house. He gave them the name of the realtor along with his address and phone number. He ended his letter by wishing them well, and that they looked forward to having them as neighbors.

Samuel and Kate read the letter and talked about it for a long time. It was finally decided that he would contact the real estate agent for more information. A few days later, the family went to the Bird-in-Hand market where they knew they would find a phone so Samuel could call the agent.

Kate and the children were walking around the market when Samuel finally found them after his call. For the first time in a long time, he looked happy. "How was your call?" she asked.

"Good, very good. But before I tell you what he said, I want you to know that I gave my name as Samuel King. I know that I don't need to, but I just don't want any questions."

"Okay," Kate said, "then I am Kate King. So tell me what he said."

"The property next to the Esh farm has twenty-five acres, a large barn with animals and equipment, a two-story house with five bedrooms and two indoor bathrooms. The price is a reasonable thirty-five thousand dollars. We could pay cash, but it would only leave us with fifteen thousand dollars in the bank. Oh, the house is furnished. The Amish couple who lived there are both dead, and they didn't have any children or relatives. If we don't like that place, he has other to show us. I'm sure we can find a place if you are willing to make the move."

"You are my husband, and I love you. I will go where you say."

"We will start making arrangements for travel. The realtor said he knows someone who will pick up us at the bus station or train station. Once I have our travel plans made and a date set, I will call him, and he will set up the driver for us."

So they started getting everything in order to make the move. The time and the date were set. Now the only thing left to do was to tell their families, inviting them to dinner the night two days before they were scheduled to leave to tell them.

The table was set, the food was cooking, the only thing to do was to wait. Kate's parents arrived just as Samuel's parents were coming over to the Dawdi house. As they all settled down to dinner, everyone was talking about the weather, the planting, and how it was nice to have winter behind them. Finally, as everyone finished their meal, Samuel said, "Kate and I wanted you to come so we could tell you of the changes that will be taking place in our lives. Day after tomorrow, we will be leaving Lancaster County to move to Troy, Pennsylvania."

Everyone was in shock.

"We have a property that we will probably purchase there. That area has a small Amish community, and the house and farm were owned by an elderly Amish couple. They both have passed away, and they didn't have any children. The house is furnished, and all the farm equipment and farm animals come with the deal.

"We hope you understand, but I can't stay here any longer. Every day is a reminder of what I have done to our families.

"One last thing, we are going to use the last name of King instead of Deitweller. This is because I don't want anyone bringing up the fire. We will take little Jacob with us and raise him as our own until Annie returns. Then we will bring him home to his mother. We ask for your support of our decision."

"Well, son, if you think this is the right thing to do, and it will bring you peace, we will support your decision. Is there anything we can do to help?" John asked.

"I really think we are all prepared to go. Kate and I are ready to start our new life in Troy, Pennsylvania."

The rest of the evening was spent talking about the move. Their parents were worried about whether they had enough money. Did they think the area would be good? Would they have access to everything that they would need? Questions—lots of questions—but by the time the parents left, they all felt comfortable with the move. Not happy, they would miss them, but they were satisfied that they would be all right.

Two days later, Samuel, Kate, Rebecca Ruth, and little Jacob boarded a train to their new life. A few short hours later, they arrived in Elmira, New York, the closest station to Troy. The driver met them as they got off the train. They got their luggage and were off to their new adventure.

It only took about an hour to reach Troy, and they enjoyed the drive, looking at all the new scenery. This area of Pennsylvania had rolling hills and valleys and was very pretty. They weren't used to the fields for planting being on a hillside. In Lancaster County, the land was mostly flat. They were pleased when the driver pulled into the drive of a farm.

"Good day, Mr. King, Mrs. King. How was your trip? Come in. I have the house all opened up and ready to look at."

The house was perfect. It was a house that would be a good fit for their family. The furnishings were old but very well taken care of. They could always change things in the future. Samuel and the agent walked the property and checked out the barn and out buildings. When they got back to the house, the agent said he would give them a few minutes to talk. When he returned, Samuel told him that they would take it. "Well, good. I have made arrangements for you to stay in the house as renters until the closing," the agent told them.

"Oh, that would be wonderful. We do need some things from the store if we stay here," Kate said.

"I have put bread, milk, and eggs in the refrigerator and some soup in the cupboard, but I would be happy to take you to Troy to the store. That way, you will know how to get there."

They all piled into the car and headed to Troy. It was a quiet little town, nothing like the Lancaster area they were used to. They went to the grocery store and picked up groceries, and then to the hardware store for kerosene for the lanterns.

When they arrived back to the house, a man was just getting out of his buggy. "Hello," he said, "I'm Benjamin Esh from the next farm down the road. I have been coming over twice a day since Jonah died to take care of the animals. Every so often, I have been coming over with my buggy and taking Jonah's horse for a run into town. That gave him some exercise. I kept the cows milked and the eggs collected. I sure hope you will like it here."

"Hi, I'm Samuel King, my wife Kate, and this is Rebecca Ruth and little Jacob. We're glad to be here."

"Where are you from?" Benjamin asked.

"Lancaster County, Pennsylvania. Not too much land available there anymore."

"I had a letter from a Samuel Deitweller about six weeks ago. He was asking all about the area and about available property. Never heard back from him. Glad you're here. Once you get settled, come over and meet my family."

"We'd like that. Thank you."

Benjamin and the agent left at the same time. The agent said he would be in touch with them in a few days. Kate started right on cleaning. First, the kitchen; once she had cleaned the kitchen completely, she made a pot of soup and put it on to simmer. Then the three bedrooms that they would be using were cleaned, and clean sheets were put on the beds.

Samuel was out in the barn, taking care of the animals and checking out the equipment. Everything was well taken care of. By 5:00 p.m., the little family sat down to eat their first meal in their new home. Once Kate and Samuel were settled into their new home, they finally found peace.

In the years that followed, there were three more children, but they never heard from Annie. Jacob grew up to be a strong, hard-working young man who had a talent for woodworking. He eventually married Sally Yoder, and they started their family. Jacob never knew that he was not Kate and Samuel's son. Since he and Rebecca had the same birthday, everyone assumed that they were twins, and Kate and Samuel never told anyone they weren't. That would have been very hard to explain and would bring up the subject of the fire again.

CHAPTER 8
Annie's New Life

When Annie left the Deitweller farm so many years ago, she had to get away from everything that reminded her of what had happened. She knew too that by leaving little Jacob with Samuel, he would be well taken care of and loved.

She first went to Lancaster. She found a small furnished apartment and quickly found a job as a waitress; but as she worked, she found that more and more Amish were coming into the restaurant, and she was afraid someone would recognize her. After she had only worked there for about six months, she decided that she needed to find a place that only the Amish that lived there would be. She didn't want an area where there would be a constant flow of outside Amish visiting the area.

After several weeks of searching, she found a place called Hummelstown, Pennsylvania. It was about an hour and fifteen minutes from Strasburg. That was a good distance from where she grew up, and it was far enough that people she would know would not just take a little drive to Hummelstown and find her. Once she got to Hummelstown, she found a job and an apartment. The apartment was upstairs from the little cafe where she worked. She loved her little apartment, and it was perfect for her.

The years went by fast. She had been in Hummelstown for about three years when one day, an Amish man came into the cafe. She was surprised because he was only the third Amish person that had come into the cafe since she started working there. He soon became a frequent visitor. They would engage in small talk when he stopped by. He was a nice guy, and she enjoyed their brief visits. Several months had gone by when he came in and asked her to go to dinner with him. "Oh, I don't know. I'm not sure I should."

"Well, you told me that you're not married. And since we are about the only Amish up this way, I thought it would be nice to get to know you better."

"Let me think on this overnight. Come in tomorrow, and I will give you an answer."

That night, Annie thought long and hard about going to dinner with him. It was just dinner, after all; they weren't courting. She had been a widow for over three years now. Maybe she did need to spend some time with someone, and she liked him. Jonathan, his name was Jonathan Lapp, was at the cafe first thing the next morning. When he walked in, Annie met him with a big smile. "So, how are you today?" he asked.

"I'm fine. I hope you are."

"Did you make up your mind?"

"Yes, I have. I would like to have dinner with you."

"Good. How about Friday night. We will go to the Warwick Hotel. They say they have good food there."

"Sounds good to me. I will see you then."

"I will pick you up at 6:00 p.m." He waved as he walked out the door, and Annie returned his wave.

Friday night finally arrived, and Annie was ready when Jonathan came to pick her up. She had just made a new dress and decided to wear that since it was a special occasion.

"Ready to go?" he asked Annie as she came out of her apartment. "All ready."

It was only a short ride in the cab to the hotel. They really didn't even have much time for conversation. Once at the hotel, they were seated and given menus. "Everything looks good," Jonathan said. "What would you like?"

"There are so many choices. I don't know what to choose. What are you going to have?"

Jonathan, still looking at the menu, said he thought he would have the pot roast. "Although the fried chicken sounds good too. So many choices and so little room in my stomach."

"I think I have decided what I want," Annie said. "I'm going to have the pork loin with sauerkraut and potatoes."

"Wow! Now the pressure is on to decide. I guess I will stick with the pot roast," Jonathan said.

As they sat waiting for the waitress to come and take their order, Annie asked Jonathan where he was from. "Oh it is a small town south of Intercourse. I'm sure that you have never heard of it."

"Well, I'm from Strasburg. Is it anywhere near there?

"Have you heard of Kinzers?" Jonathan asked.

"Of course. What are you doing up here?" Annie asked him.

"Well, I had a dispute with my oldest brother over some property, and I left. It was probably a cowardly thing to do, but I did it. How about you? Why are you so far from Strasburg?"

"I guess you could say I too took the coward's way out."

"What happened?" Jonathan asked. "If you don't mind my asking."

"I haven't talked to anyone about this. I was married to a wonderful man. Jacob Deitweller. He was a good husband and father. One day about four years ago, he was working in his father's barn, putting in the hay. He was up in the hayloft stacking bales when his brother left the loft to help his father with the next wagon. As Samuel, Jacob's brother, went down the ladder, a barn cat tripped him, and he lost his balance. When he lost his balance, he knocked over a lantern, which immediately caught the hay on the floor of the barn on fire. The fire spread so fast that Jacob was trapped in the loft. He was burned to death in the fire.

"After the fire, I was in such a state of shock that I couldn't function. I couldn't eat or sleep. I just sat in the rocking chair that Jacob made for me and stared at the wall.

"At his funeral, I made a fool of myself by lashing out at his brother Samuel. I told him that it was his fault that Jacob was dead, and I never wanted to set eyes on him again. I told him since he had killed my husband, he had killed me. I was terrible to him.

"After the funeral, I went back to my house and again locked everyone out, even my son, who was a few months old. That night, I packed my things and walked away from everything and everyone.

I left a note telling Samuel that he could raise my son. He is married to my sister. I'm not proud of what I did. I was just not in my right mind. I wouldn't blame you if you decided that you did not want to spend time with someone who would walk away from her family."

"I think I can somewhat understand. You were just so consumed with grief that you didn't really know what you were doing. I remember hearing about that fire. It isn't very often that someone loses his life in a fire. Have you tried to contact your family?" Jonathan asked.

"No. Now I am so ashamed of how I acted that I'm afraid to get in touch. It has been four years since the accident, and I have not forgiven myself. How can anyone else forgive me for leaving?"

"Annie, you have to forgive yourself before you will be able to receive forgiveness from others. Do you miss your son?" he asked.

"Yes, very much. I think about him all the time."

Just as Annie said that, their food arrived and they ate their meals.

"Jonathan, do you have more than one brother?" Annie asked.

"I am the youngest of fifteen. I have ten brothers and four sisters. My dispute was with my oldest brother. You know that the Amish way is for the parental farm to go to the youngest son. Well, my brother wanted it. He went to my father, but Father held true to our ways and told him no. Benjamin, that's my brother, kept making trouble, and I finally had it out with him. I was tired of fighting. They don't know where I am either."

"Well, aren't we a couple of lost souls?"

"It may be a good thing we found each other. We can be outcasts together," Jonathan said.

As they were finishing their meal, they decided to take a walk before they called for a cab. For the rest of the evening, they talked about how they ended up in the same place after leaving their families. Jonathan dropped Annie off at her apartment, saying he would see her the next week.

That was how their relationship started, two lost souls finding comfort in each other. They started seeing each other more often. They had dinner together about once a week. Sometimes, Annie cooked for him; sometimes, they went out to eat; and sometimes, they just ordered pizza and ate it at Annie's apartment. Their relationship went on that way for the next two years, feeling comfortable with each other, neither one judging the other for leaving their families.

Finally, Jonathan arrived one night at Annie's for dinner and was acting very strange. She asked what was wrong but didn't force the issue when he just shrugged his shoulders. After some time had gone by, he looked at Annie and said, "I have something I need to ask you. Will you marry me?"

"Jonathan, I didn't expect that. You know what? I will marry you. I know we will be very happy together."

A few weeks later, they found a bishop who would marry them. It was a very small affair compared to Annie's first wedding. It was the bishop, two deacons, witnesses, and Annie and Jonathan.

To save money, Jonathan moved into Annie's apartment over the cafe. He had been living in a boarding house. They were soon settled into a routine, saving as much as they could so someday they could buy a farm. Jonathan always watched the properties for sale in the Strasburg and Kinzer areas. They had been married for about six months when Annie told Jonathan that she was pregnant. He was overjoyed and looking forward to being a father.

As time passed, the family grew. Three more children were born to the couple; they were Daniel, David, Sarah, and Amos. Amos was about two years old when one night, Jonathan said that there was a farm for sale on Belmont Road between Strasburg and Kinzers. "I talked to the agent, and we have saved enough money to buy it. It comes with all the farm equipment, animals, and house furnishings. What do you think? Isn't it about time that we reconnect with our families?"

This is what they had been saving for, and it was time to get back to their families, mend the fences, and let their families get to know their children. "I say buy it. Let's go home," Annie said.

One month later, they signed final papers on the farm and moved in. Annie went to work cleaning and making the house theirs. Jonathan was busy in the barn, getting it the way he wanted it.

They needed to get the children in school so the following Monday morning, they took the children to the closest one-room schoolhouse. Annie and Jonathan got them settled and left.

"What are your names?" the teacher asked.

"I'm Daniel Lapp, and these are my brother and sister David and Sarah. They are Lapps too. We have one other brother at home, Amos, but he is too young to come to school."

One of the children spoke up and said his name was Jonathan Lapp. "Are we related?" he asked.

"Probably not," and with that, Daniel took his seat.

A couple of nights later, after they had finished dinner and were settling down for Bible reading, there was a knock at the door. Answering it, Jonathan immediately recognized the bishop from his old church district. "I don't mean to barge in, but I wanted to come and welcome you to the church district and tell you that Sunday service will be at Abner Lapp's farm next week. I am Bishop Zimmerman."

"Hello, bishop, please come in. I am Jonathan Lapp."

The bishop looked at him close, "We used to have a Jonathan Lapp at our church, but he left a long time ago."

"Well, bishop, he's back. I would like you to meet my wife Annie, our sons Daniel, David, and Amos, and our daughter Sarah."

"I thought you looked familiar when you opened the door. Where have you been all these years, son?"

"I have been living and working in Hummelstown. There are only a few Amish up there, but we attended services regularly," Jonathan explained.

"Well, son, it is good to have you back. Have you seen much of your family yet?" the bishop asked.

"No, and I would appreciate it if you did not say anything about us being back. We are still settling in and have plans to visit this coming Sunday."

"Fine, I won't tell anyone you're back."

A short time later, the bishop left, and Annie and Jonathan headed to bed. "I guess we should go to visit your family on Friday," Jonathan said.

"Okay. As soon as the children get home from school."

On Friday afternoon, Jonathan, Annie, and Amos were waiting to leave when the children got home from school. They were all settled in the family buggy and headed to the King farm. "Who are these people we are going to see?" Daniel asked.

"They are your grandparents. My parents," Annie said.

"Oh, I can't wait to be at their house and meet them," Daniel said.

The closer the buggy got to her childhood home, the more nervous Annie got. By the time they got to the drive, she had broken out in a cold sweat. Jonathan sensed her nerves and held her hand. "It will be fine."

When he pulled the buggy to a stop, a man emerged from the barn. Jonathan got out and helped Annie down. She started to walk toward her father. When he suddenly stopped. He looked closer at her. "Annie, is that you?" By now, her father was running across the drive, smiling. When he reached Annie, he wrapped his arms around her. "Oh, Annie, we have missed you so."

Mary, seeing the buggy that had come into their drive, came out of the house. She looked and realized that it was Annie. "Oh, oh, Annie, my Annie. Where have you been? We have missed you so much."

Soon, Joseph, Annie's brother, now a grown man, came out of the barn. When he saw who it was, he too ran to her. "Sister, welcome home." It was Joseph who noticed that there was someone with her. "Who is this?" he asked.

"Oh, Mama, Papa, Joseph, I want you to meet my husband, Jonathan Lapp, and these are our children Daniel, David, Sarah, and Amos."

"Welcome. Look at these children. Would you like a snack?" Mary asked. "Come into the house, all of you. I'll put a pot of coffee on, and we will have some shoofly pie."

That afternoon was spent with many questions about where she had been all these years. How had she survived? How had she met Jonathan? Where was he from? And on and on and on. Finally, it was her turn to ask questions. "How is little Jacob?"

"He is doing well. He lives with Kate and Samuel, but they do not live here anymore. They moved to Troy, Pennsylvania. Samuel just could not deal with the loss of his brother and then you taking off and feeling guilty. He was very depressed, so they decided to start fresh. They moved to Troy, Pennsylvania, and have taken the last name of King.

"They were able to purchase property there and are very happy. Samuel and Jacob have a very profitable woodworking business. They have also raised Rebecca and little Jacob as twins. People just assumed that they were, and Kate and Samuel did not tell them any different.

"We miss them very much, but they are happy, and that is what is important."

"I am so sorry for my part in that. I didn't know what I was doing."

"We all know that, even Samuel."

It was getting close to the dinner hour, and Mary insisted that they stay for dinner. Annie and her mother got busy preparing the meal while everyone else, except Sarah, went to the barn. Mary prepared meat loaf, mashed potatoes, fresh green beans, apple sauce, chowchow, and bread and butter.

When the meal was completed and the dishes were cleaned up, Annie and her family said their goodbyes and headed for home. They had discussed the property that Jonathan and Annie had purchased, and they were happy for them. "We live so close, you can come and visit often," Annie said.

As they rode home, Jonathan said to Annie, "That went well."

"Yes it did. It is good to be home."

Jonathan's turn to be nervous came a couple days later. As they started down Kinzer Road, beads of sweat broke out on his forehead. Finally, they arrived at his parents' home. There were several buggies parked in the yard. He stopped the buggy, and they all got out. As they knocked on the door, they were wondering what was going on. The door was answered by his sister Mary Ann. "Jonathan! Is that really you?"

"Yes, it is. I have come home, and I brought my wife and children."

"Oh, Jonathan, you couldn't have come at a better time. Father is ill. Just yesterday, he said he wanted to see you one more time. Now you're here. Come in, come in."

As they entered the kitchen, he saw a lot of familiar faces, but it was his mother that he focused on. "Mama, it's Jonathan. I've come home."

"Oh, my baby, my baby," she said as she got up and walked toward him.

"I'm sorry that I left, but now I've come home. Can I see Father?"

"No, you don't belong here anymore," his brother Benjamin said.

"You just wait a minute, Benjamin. This is still my house, and I say who can be here and who can't. It was your attitude that drove him away before, and I will not let that happen again. Now let me take you to your father," she said.

As they entered the room, Marian said, "Seth, look who has come home. Our baby Jonathan."

"Jonathan, son, I have missed you so much. I am so glad you have come home. I hope you will stay."

"Yes, Father, and I have a wife and four grandchildren for you."

"Marian, would you please get Benjamin, Seth, John, and Mary Ann to come in here. I have something to say, and I want witnesses."

When Jonathan's siblings had entered the room, his father began to speak. "I am settling this problem with the land once and for all. It is Amish tradition that the youngest son inherits the family property, and that is the way it will be in this family. Benjamin, you bullied your brother before he left, and that was the reason he left. That will not happen again. The property is Jonathan's. Do you understand, Benjamin?"

"Yes."

"Mary Ann?"

"Yes."

"Seth?"

"Yes."

"John?"

"Yes, as it should be."

"Now, I want to visit with my son that has been gone for so long and hear all about his fraa and my grandchildren."

Everyone left the room, and Jonathan and his father talked for a long time. When Jonathan finally left the room, he found his wife and children talking in the kitchen with his mother and Seth. The children were talking nonstop with Seth, Anne, and his mother. Jonathan was so happy to see how they were getting along that he was filled with joy that he had finally come home.

Benjamin left after the meeting with his father. He was a very bitter person. Questions filled his head. Why was he born first instead of last? Why did Jonathan get the property? He needed that property to make a living for his family. No one knew what Benjamin would be up to next, but Jonathan and his family would soon find out.

Back at the Lapp farm, Jonathan and his family were saying their goodbyes to his mother and headed home. When they arrived, there was a buggy in his yard. Benjamin was sitting on the porch. As Jonathan got out of the buggy, he asked, "How can I help you?"

"I want to have it out with you here and now. That property is mine. I am the oldest, and I deserve to have it," he said.

"You heard Father. I inherit the land, house, and barn with all the equipment and livestock. Why are you so upset about me getting the property? I don't understand. Explain it to me."

"I deserve the property. It is mine, and I won't let you take it." With that, Benjamin left the porch and ran to his buggy. When he got to the buggy, he reached in the back seat and pulled something out. Jonathan could not see what it was. Benjamin then ran to the barn with Jonathan right behind him. By the time he got there, Benjamin had already started the fire. In such a short period of time, the fire was out of control. Jonathan was in the barn and saw Benjamin standing by the back door of the barn smiling. It was then that Jonathan could hear Annie in the yard screaming for him. He could not stay in the barn and take a chance of another fire accident for her to deal with, so he quickly left the barn and joined his family on the lawn. They stood there and watched the barn burn. In the background, they could hear the sirens of the firemen coming.

By the time the firefighters were finished, the barn was totally destroyed. The fire chief came over to the family to ask some questions. "Do you know how the fire got started?" he asked.

Jonathan replied to the question, "My brother started it. He ran in, started the fire, but he didn't come back out this door. I don't know if he got out the other door or not."

"So he may still be in the barn?" the fire chief asked.

He hollered to his men that there may be a victim in there. "Let's keep checking."

The firefighters began looking for a body. In the meantime, the fire chief called the coroner to come to the scene. All the time, the firefighters continued looking through the destroyed barn, looking for Benjamin's body. Buggies soon started to arrive at the Lapp farm. Some of the people they knew, others they did not know, but they were all concerned. A short time later, Jonathan's sister and her husband arrived. "Are you all right?" she asked as she was getting out of the buggy. "What started the fire?"

"Benjamin was here when we got home. He said he wanted to have it out with me once and for all. He said that he deserved the property more than I did. I told him that what Father said was final, and that was the end of it. He was furious and ran to his buggy and took something out of it and headed to the barn. The next thing we knew, the barn was on fire. The really bad part is he never came out of the barn. They are looking for him, but have not found his body yet."

Soon, there were so many buggies parked in their yard that they could hardly walk around. It is amazing how a group of people who don't have phones are able to spread the word about things going on in the area so fast. The fire department finally left, but the police and coroner were still there looking for Benjamin when Mary Ann said, "There is Benjamin walking up the drive."

The police officer walked up to him and asked if he had set the fire? "No, why would I do that?"

From behind his parents, Daniel spoke up, "He started the fire. I saw him do it."

With that little bit of information, the officer was about to arrest Benjamin, but Jonathan stopped him. "I will not press charges. We will handle it our own way."

Mary Ann walked over to her brother. "How could you do this? And to your own brother. You heard Father. It is Jonathan's farm and land. That is the Amish way. You need to ask Jonathan's forgiveness. You have cost him a lot of money."

"Never. I will never apologize to him."

"Then let it be known that you are no longer welcome in our home. Your wife and children may come, but you may not. When we leave here, Jonah and I are going to the homestead and will tell Mother and Father what you have done here. Goodbye, Benjamin, and may God be with you because you have burned so many bridges that no one else will be."

Jonah and Mary Ann left and went to her parents' home to inform them what had happened. Seth and Marion could not believe what Mary Ann was telling them. "I have told Benjamin he is longer welcome at our home. Mary and the children are always welcome but not him."

"I need to talk to Benjamin. I don't understand why he has so much hate in his heart for Jonathan. I don't know if he ever even liked him. Benjamin was twenty when Jonathan was born. I just don't understand," Seth said.

Several weeks later, the community came together for a barn raising at the Lapp farm. One person whose absence was noticed by most everyone was Benjamin. His wife and children came. When Mary got to Jonathan's farm, she went straight to him and told him how sorry she was for the trouble Benjamin had caused.

"Mary, you do not have to apologize for him. He needs to do that on his own. I don't know why he dislikes me so, but I love him, and I forgive him."

The barn raising was a complete success. By seven that night, the last shingles were placed on the roof. Everyone had worked hard and were tired by the time it was done. Annie and Jonathan thanked everyone and said goodbye.

Over the next few weeks, Jonathan's fathers health improved, and the family gathered often. Benjamin did not go to church or any family get together. He never visited his parents or went anywhere. He just worked his farm. He continued to be a bitter, lonely man for the rest of his life.

And so life went on for Annie's family. She wrote to Kate often, but they decided not to tell Jacob that he was not Kate and Samuel's son. All the years that Annie was away, she kept a journal. She told Jonathan about the journal and asked that when it was her time to go home to be with the Lord, to pass it on to Jacob.

CHAPTER 9
Jacob's Story

Life was good for Kate, Samuel, and their children in Troy. Their neighbors on each side were Amish and had many children. There was always someone to play with. Hours were spent running around the woods that connected the three properties. During the day, when chores were done, the boys would run around and play. But after dinner, the boys and girls from all three families would play hide-and-seek or catch lightning bugs.

Jacob's year of growing up were happy ones, but he also sensed that he was different. It wasn't because Kate and Samuel treated him any different; it was just a sense he had. As he was growing, he would spend many hours in Samuel's woodshop. Samuel taught him about all the tools and how to use them. When Samuel was working on a piece of furniture, Jacob was always there watching. As he watched, he asked many questions about what Samuel was doing and why.

Samuel gave Jacob scrap wood to practice on. Samuel got a kick out of watching him do the things that he did, so by the time Jacob was done with his schooling, he had developed some fine woodworking skills. So good that Samuel asked him to come to work for him.

As the years passed, the two men had built a profitable business. There were people from all over the country that would order pieces of their handwork. Kate and Samuel's three other sons were not interested in working with the wood. They preferred to farm and work with the soil. This was a win-win situation for the King family. While Samuel and Jacob worked in the shop, creating wonderful pieces of furniture, the other boys were running a profitable farm.

In the fall of the year that Rebecca and Jacob turned twenty, a customer from a place called Owego, New York, came to see them about doing some extensive cabinet work. This customer would change the lives of the King family again. The customer was Jason Miller. He had written a letter to Samuel and told him what he needed. He said he would be down to their shop to discuss the project the following Wednesday. Samuel and Jacob talked for hours about the job, but they were not sure if they could do such a big one but decided to wait and talk to Mr. Miller when he came.

Jason arrived at the shop at ten on a Wednesday morning in October. He was driven by a man in a uniform. Because Samuel and Jacob had never seen a chauffeur or a limo, they didn't know that it was a sign of true wealth. But when Jason stepped from the car, he was dressed in jeans and a sports shirt. Entering the shop, he said, "Good morning, I am Jason Miller."

"Good morning, I am Samuel King, and this is my son Jacob King. Welcome to our shop."

The three men sat down and started talking about the job. Kate had seen Mr. Miller's car pull in and decided to make some cinnamon rolls to take out to them. A short time later, she appeared at the door with a pot of coffee and some cinnamon rolls. "I don't mean to interrupt, but I have brought some coffee and rolls. I hope you will enjoy them. I will take some out to your driver."

"Mr. Miller, this is my wife, Kate King."

"How do you do, Mrs. King?"

"It is nice to meet you, Mr. Miller."

Kate took some rolls and coffee to Mr. Miller's driver on her way back to the house. The men continued their conversation for another hour and a half. Miller explained that his new business needed cabinets built for all the offices, ten in all. "The cabinets would be about ten feet long and would be your basic cabinets with drawers and doors and a knee space in the center so someone could sit at it to use a computer."

During the discussion, they decided that it would be best if they were built in the King shop and shipped to Owego. They discussed what kind of wood they would use for the project. Samuel showed

Jason some examples of the style of cabinets that may work for his purposes. The decision was made that five of the cabinets would be made of oak, and five would be made of cherry. The oak ones would be a little less formal with simple drawer pulls and hinges. The cherry ones would have fancier pulls and hinges.

"Now for my office," Jason said. "I need a ceiling-to-floor wall unit with open shelves and areas with doors. The base will need to have drawers all the way across that are file-size. I would also like a large matching desk. The only thing is that when you build my unit, you will need to build it on site.

"Here is my proposal. Once you get the ten units done, I will come down and get you to come up and look at my office. That way, you will have some idea of what the next project will be. If you are still willing to do that build, I will provide a place for you to stay and all the equipment that you will need to do the job. I will also provide someone to do your cooking, prepare your lunches, and clean the apartment for you. The apartment will only be a block from the work site, so you will be able to walk back and forth each day. I will give you a key to the building so you can start as early as you like.

"Let's see. Have I covered everything? Oh, one more thing. My driver will pick you up on Monday morning and drop you off at the work site. And every Friday, he will bring you back home to your family for the weekend. Do you have any questions?"

"Wow, that gives us much to think about. First, we will go pick up the wood for the first unit this afternoon and get started on those. We will get one unit done and have it ready for you to approve of before we start on the rest. Then we will go from there."

"That sounds good to me," Jason said. "Now we need to talk money. I will give you a check today for ten thousand dollars so you will be able to get started with the materials and anything else you will need. Anytime you find you need money for supplies, just let me know.

"For every unit that you complete, I will pay you each five thousand dollars. For my unit, I will pay you each fifteen thousand. Is that agreeable with both of you?"

"That is more than enough, but let's wait and see if you like our work before you offer so much."

"Your woodworking skills have come highly recommended by several people. I've seen the quality of your work, and I want nothing but the best, so I came to you."

Once all the discussions were over and Jason was ready to leave, they shook hands on the deal. "We will contact you when we have the first one done. Can you leave a business card with us so we have the number to call you?"

"Very good. I look forward to hearing from you." And with that, Jason left.

Samuel and Jacob stood looking at each other for several minutes, neither one speaking. Finally, Samuel found his voice. "I can hardly believe that. That's a lot of money, and I guess we have our work cut out for us. I guess we better go have lunch and then go to the lumberyard. We have to get enough wood to make the first unit. When we see how long it takes us, then we can make arrangements for the yard to make deliveries when we are ready for more lumber. I'll call the driver and ask him to pick us up around 2:00 p.m. That should give us enough time to make a diagram and make a list of supplies."

"Yeah. With the two of us, we should be able to get everything in one trip. Maybe if we get to the lumberyard early enough, they will be able to get the materials delivered tomorrow."

They talked nonstop during lunch, telling Kate and the rest of the family about their conversation with Mr. Miller. "He has proposed paying us more money than we ever thought of. He has ordered ten units, five in oak and five in cherry. We will make one and have him come to look at it. Once he has approved, then we will make the rest of them. He has given us a check to buy the first of the materials we will need. He is paying for all the materials and then paying us each for the labor to make them.

"Once we have the first ten units done, we will go to Owego, New York, to make a floor-to-ceiling unit for his office, along with a desk to match. He will have all the equipment to build that unit all set up in his warehouse. He will also have an apartment for us, one block from the work site, with someone to clean and cook for us.

"Best of all, we will be picked up on Monday morning, and we will be brought home on Friday afternoon for the weekend. It is amazing that he is doing this because of our work."

The rest of the meal, the family discussed the new adventure. After lunch, Samuel and Jacob were out in the shop, making sure that they had everything on their list that you would need to do the job. At 2:00 p.m., the driver arrived to take them to the lumberyard; and by the time they got home, they had ordered everything that they would need, and it would be delivered the next day.

After having a cup of coffee, Jacob said he was going to the shop to go over their tools to make sure everything was in good shape to do a good job. Samuel went too; and by the time it was getting dark, the shop was clean, and everything was ready to start their project. "It is good that we didn't have any big orders on the book. Now we can just concentrate on this one," Jacob said.

"Yeah, I was a little worried about our lack of work when I got Mr. Miller's letter. If we do a good job, we won't have to worry about work for a while. This may lead to other jobs," Samuel said.

At seven the next morning, the lumber and supplies were delivered, and Samuel and Jacob were starting their work. They worked steady for several hours when Kate brought out their lunch. "It is good to take a break," Jacob said. "We have already made some progress with the first unit." They showed Kate how much they had done.

By the time they closed the shop that night, they had made quite a bit of progress. Walking to the house, Samuel slapped Jacob on the back and told him that he was proud of him. He had done a good job. So for the next several days, their work progressed, and the unit was really coming together. They figured that by the middle of the following week, they would be calling Mr. Miller to come down.

One day they were in the shop when Kate came to the door. "Samuel, can I speak to you?" She waited outside for Samuel to come out. Seeing the distress in his wife's eyes, he hurried out to see what was wrong. "I have just received a letter from Annie. She has come back home, and she has a new husband and four children Daniel,

David, Sarah, and Amos. They have purchased a farm on Belmont Road, only a mile from where my parents live. The first part of the letter was written to you. Here, read it."

> Samuel, please forgive me. I know now that you were not responsible for Jacob's death. It was an accident. I only hope that someday you will be able to forgive me for the way I treated you. When I left my son in your care, I knew down deep inside that you are a good man, and you would raise him and love him as your own. I hear that he has grown into a wonderful young man. I thank you for that.
>
> I have learned that you and Kate have taken the last name of King, and I understand that too. I owe you and Kate a great debt. I don't know if I can ever repay you, but I do thank you.
>
> I also have been told that you never told Jacob that he and Rebecca Ruth were actually cousins and not twins. I understand the reason behind that. I know that if you tried to explain it to people, they may not understand the situation, and most people would not understand a mother leaving her son and going away. You did what would make life easier for you and your family.
>
> I just want you to know, Samuel, I love you and Kate for what you have done. I hope that someday we will get the opportunity to be together, and your children can meet their Aunt Annie.

After Samuel had finished reading the letter, he turned to Kate and said, "I always knew that she would come back and forgive me." With that, he turned and went back into the shop.

Once he went back into the shop, he couldn't put the letter out of his mind. He also wondered if he and Kate should tell Jacob and the children the whole story. Would that create upheaval? He decided that he and Kate would have to think long and hard about that.

The next day, Kate came hurrying into the shop after coming home from the store and said, "We have a new family in the community. Their names are Miller, and I just met the mother and daughter. Sarah Miller is the mother and the daughter is Sally. They will be at the church service on Sunday. Jacob, you should make sure that Sally knows about the young people's gathering on Sunday night. See you with your lunch shortly." And she was out the door and headed to the house.

Jacob and Samuel looked at each other and started to laugh. Kate was very excited about this new family.

Sunday morning was busy with chores, breakfast, and getting the food packed for the common meal following the service. Kate was excited about the new family. She had enjoyed her visit with Sarah and was looking forward to spending more time with her today. Jacob, on the other hand, wasn't looking forward to meeting Sally. His mother told him that she was about his age and quite cute, but that doesn't always hold true. Sometimes, mothers think some girls are cuter than they really are.

When they arrived at the Yoder farm for the service, there was a large group of people standing in the front yard. Everyone wanted to get to know the Millers.

The Sunday service started just after the Kings arrived. Jacob had not been introduced to the new family yet, but during the service, he found himself watching Sally Miller. "She is pretty, just like Mama had said." She had light-brown hair and hazel eyes. She did appear to be about his age, and he wondered if she had willingly moved from Ohio, or was she unhappy about the move? Did she have a boyfriend back in Ohio that she was missing? There were lots of questions in his mind, and he wondered if he would get to find out the answers.

After the service was over and the meal had been served, the people gathered around to socialize and play games. Jacob finally had an opportunity to introduce himself to Sally. "Hi, Sally, I'm Jacob

King. You met my mother the other day at the store. How do you like Troy?"

"It is a lot smaller than the community we came from, but I do like it, and I think it will be a good place to live."

"Tonight, there will be a young people's gathering. Are you planning on going?" Jacob asked.

"I really hadn't given it much thought. I didn't think that I will know anyone there. Are you going?"

"I'll be there, and so will my sister and brothers. You can ride with us if you want. I'm sure we could squeeze one more person in the buggy. If you want to think about it, just let me know.

"Have you met my sister Rebecca Ruth or my brothers yet? You'll like them. They're a lot of fun.

"Just let me know about tonight before you leave. If I am going to pick you up, I will need to know where you live." With that Jacob walked away to let her think.

Sally watched Jacob walk away. He must be about her age. He is cute with that dark hair and blue eyes. "I really think I would like to get to know him better."

That night, after chores were done, Jacob, Rebecca Ruth, and the boys headed to the Miller farm to pick up Sally. She was waiting on the front porch; and when she saw their buggy, she hurried down the steps. Jacob introduced her to everyone as she climbed in. Then they were off for a fun evening.

When they arrived back at the Yoder's farm, there were several buggies already there. As they entered the barn, groups of young people were standing around. Rebecca and Sally headed off to the group of girls while the boys all went in different directions.

Within a few minutes, the singing began and then a lively game of soft ball. Sometime later, Mrs. Yoder served refreshments. It was a fun night, and everyone had a good time. Rebecca and Sally really got along well and planned to get together soon.

After dropping Sally off at home, Jacob took quite a bit of teasing from his brothers. "She is pretty cute. When are you going to dump us and start taking her home by yourself?" On and on they went until they finally pulled into their yard.

"Just for the way you have teased me all the way, you two can take care of the horse and buggy," Jacob said as he hopped down and headed toward the back door with Rebecca.

Rebecca and Jacob found their parents sitting at the kitchen table, having a cup of coffee. "Did you have fun?" their mother asked. "How about Sally? Did you meet everyone and have a good time?"

"I think we all had a good time, and Sally met lots of people. I really think she and I will become good friends," Rebecca said.

"Well, I'm off to bed. Tomorrow, I would like to get the finish work done on Mr. Miller's cabinet so we can call him to get the final approval. What do you think, Father?"

"That sounds like it is a good plan. The sooner we get approval, the sooner we can get started on the rest of the job," Samuel said. "Now I'm off to bed too."

Once Kate had rinsed out their coffee cups, she headed to bed.

By 3:00 p.m. the next day, the cabinet was ready for inspection. They had worked hard to do their best work ever. Samuel went to the phone and called Jason Miller. Jason answered his phone. "Mr. King, it's good to hear from you. How is everything going?"

"Everything is fine. I'm calling to let you know we have the first cabinet done and ready for your inspections."

"Already? That was fast work. Since today is Monday, how about it if I come down on Wednesday morning?" Jason asked.

"That would be fine."

"Okay, see you then, and thank you, Mr. King."

Being confident that Mr. Miller would approve of their work, they decided to make the cuts for the next cabinet. By Tuesday night, all the cuts had been made, and they were ready to start assembling the next cabinet.

Wednesday morning, Mr. Miller arrived at ten. As he entered the shop, he spotted the completed cabinet set off to the side of the shop. After he greeted Samuel and Jacob, he went to check it out closer. He looked at it for a long time, walking around it and looking close at every detail. He opened and closed the drawers and doors. He finally turned to Samuel and Jacob and said, "It is the finest piece of workmanship I have seen in a long time. After seeing this, I know I made the right decision in coming to you."

"Thank you for your confidence in us," Samuel said. "If you are satisfied, we will start working on the next four in oak. We will call when we have those done so you can send a truck to pick them up because we won't be able to store all of them. We'll make the first of the cherry ones and have you come and look at that one so you can give us your approval, if that is all right with you?"

"That sounds great. You have done fine work, and I will tell my friends about your skills."

By the first of January, Samuel and Jacob had completed the other four cabinets and were ready to have Mr. Miller come to look at the first of the cherry ones. The last week in January, Jason showed up with a truck to take the cabinets back to Owego. Once the oak cabinets were loaded on the truck, Jason came in to look at the cherry one. "This is even better than the oak ones. I give my approval to move forward with the construction of the rest of the cherry ones."

Now that winter was in full swing, the young people's gatherings were mostly spent inside family barns where large propane heaters were in place to warm the area. But sometimes, there would be ice-skating or a hayride. When they did one of those outside events, there would be a big bonfire with hot dogs and marshmallows to roast. Sally Miller and Jacob King seemed to always end up together. They enjoyed each other's company and were becoming good friends.

That year, Valentine's Day fell on the Saturday night before a church service. Jacob had been thinking about asking Sally out to dinner. He had realized a few weeks ago that he felt more for Sally than just friends. He thought that she felt the same way, but he wasn't quite sure. If they were alone together, maybe they could discuss whether they were friends or more than friends.

One night after dinner, he decided to take a ride over to the Miller's to ask her. It was a week and a half before Valentine's Day. When he knocked on the Miller's door, Sarah answered the door. "Jacob, come in. It is a cold night to be out riding. Is everything all right?"

"Yes, I just wanted to talk to Sally. Is she home?"

"Yes, come in, and I will call her." Sarah called Sally; and while Jacob waited for Sally to appear, Sarah poured him a cup of coffee and cut a slice of shoofly pie—his favorite.

When Sally came into the kitchen, Sarah excused herself. "Jacob, are you all right? It is a terrible night to be out traveling around."

"I wanted to come and ask you something. Ugh, Sally, would you go out to dinner with me next Saturday night? There is a place in Nichols that we could go to. It will be a little ride but not too bad."

"Jacob, I would love to. It will be fun to spend some time alone together. Usually, there are other people around. Thank you, and I will look forward to it."

"I will pick you up around 5:30 p.m. If it is cold, I will have a driver take us. But one way or another, we'll go have a nice meal."

Jacob stayed a little longer, enjoying the hot coffee and pie. On the ride home, Jacob was on cloud nine. He really liked Sally and had thought many times about her being his wife. By the time he got home, everyone was in bed. He made his way to his room, but sleep would not come easy tonight; he was too excited about taking Sally out.

Valentine's Day dawned clear and beautiful but extremely cold. Jacob decided it was too cold to take the buggy, so he called Caleb Jamison to see if he could drive them to Nichols. Jacob explained to him what he had planned and where they were going. "Well, Jacob, normally I would say no because I have a date, but that's where we are going, so you and your date can ride along with us. What time are your reservations for?"

"At 7:00 p.m.," Jacob replied. "I told Sally I would pick her up at 5:30 p.m., thinking that we would be taking the buggy. But if we are riding in the car, it won't take as long. What time do you think we need to leave?"

"I think if we leave by 6:15, that will get us there in time."

"Okay, that sounds good. I will get in touch with Sally to let her know," Jacob said.

"I'll pick you up at 6:00 p.m., then we will get Sally. I'll pick my date up before I get you."

"Sounds great. See you later."

Caleb and his date were good company on the ride to Nichols. Once they arrived there, the two couples went their separate ways. When they were seated, Sally looked around. "This is a nice place."

"I have only heard of it. I have never been here before. I hope the food is good," Jacob said.

Once they had placed their order, they sat, talking while they waited for their food to come. They talked about everything from the young people's gathering the following night to the weather. Sally finally asked how his work was going. "Do you have enough to keep you busy?"

"We have been working on a very large order for a businessman in Owego, New York. He ordered ten units, five in oak and five in cherry. The units are ten feet long with door and drawers when we get them done. We have the oak ones done, and they have been delivered. We're working on the cherry ones.

"When we get them done, then we start on the big project. Dad and I will be going to Owego every Monday, and we will come home every Friday night. We are making a very big wall unit and desk that need to be built on site. The man we are doing the work for is setting up and paying for an apartment for us to live in during the week with a cook and housecleaning service. They will make our lunches and have dinner ready when we get home at night.

"We are not sure how long it will take, but he is being very generous with the money that he is paying us."

"Wow, that sounds like quite a project. But you say you will be home every weekend? I will miss knowing that you are not just a mile or so away."

"I will miss you, but I will see you when I come home. I was hoping that you would be willing to wait for me and not go out with anyone else. I have really come to be quite fond of you and want to spend more time with you."

"I am so glad to hear that, Jacob, because I want to spend more time with you too."

By 8:30 p.m., they had finished their meal and were ready to leave when Caleb and his date came to their table.

Two weeks later, Jacob said goodbye when he drove her home after the young people's gathering on Sunday night. He told her they would be leaving in the morning.

Mr. Miller had a two-bedroom, two-bath apartment for them. The shop had been set up, and it had every tool they could possibly need or want. He had also made arrangements with William's Lumber mill to supply all the wood that they would need. Samuel went right to work, taking measurements and making design plans to show to Jason the next day.

Jacob and Samuel were at the office the next day at 6:00 a.m. going over their plans, their measurements, and making the order for William's Lumber. By the time Jason Miller came in, they had everything ready to show him. Once the order was placed, they set about getting ready to start their work. On Tuesday, after all the materials and supplies were delivered, they were busy organizing everything.

The next morning they were at the office at 6:00 a.m. again and had started working. The next couple of weeks were busy; but on the weekends, it was good to be home. Every weekend, Jacob would go to see Sally. They talked about everything that was going on at home and in Owego. "Tell me about Owego," Sally said one day.

"It is a nice town. There are a lot of large very old homes. The shopping area is all small privately owned stores, and I don't think there is a mall there. You would like it."

By the end of April, they had completed the last unit for Miller. With the completion of Miller's work came orders from several other businessmen in the area who had seen and heard about the Kings' work and wanted some of the fine-quality furnishings too.

When they arrived home that last Friday night, they were met with a celebration. Kate had invited Sally to join the family. She thought that they may be planning for a wedding come November. She had seen the relationship between Jacob and Sally had continued to grow and was very happy about it. She did, however, keep her thoughts to herself. She didn't want to rush things.

As Samuel and Jacob stepped out of the limo, they were happy to see everyone there. Even Sally was there for the celebration. Jacob was surprised and happy to see her. "I am so happy to see you," Jacob said to her as she walked toward him.

"Come inside. We have a wonderful dinner ready for you," Kate said. "I have had much help with the meal. Rebecca and Sally have been working all day to have this wonderful meal for you. They even baked some shoofly pie for dessert."

They went inside, and dinner was served. There were lots of questions from the family about the work they had done. One question was if they had received any orders from people who had seen the work they had done for Mr. Miller. Samuel pulled out a stack of orders from his pocket. "These are the orders that we have from other businessmen in the area and from some of Mr. Miller's friends. We will have enough work to keep us busy for some time.

"Wow, that is wonderful," Kate said.

Samuel spent many hours out in the workshop, designing and preparing material lists for the orders they had received. The orders would be done in the order that they had been received. Samuel and Jacob were busy, and the orders continued to come in.

As busy as they were, Jacob still found time to court Sally. Jacob was saving his money and talked to Samuel about building a house on top of the hill behind their house. Samuel told him that he would gift an acre to him. He was proud of the work that Jacob had done and wanted to let him know how much he appreciated him.

Sometimes, at their lunch break, they would do some drawings for a house. As they worked, they would often talk about the house. After their conversations, they would modify the plans—sometimes a lot, and sometimes just a little—each time making it better than it had been before.

In the first part of June, the architect they had hired to draw up the plans completed them and brought them to look at. By the end of June, the cellar was dug, and the foundation was laid. The building was progressing by leaps and bounds.

Jacob asked Sally to go to dinner with him in the beginning of July. This time, they would go into Wyalusing to the hotel dining room. He wanted to make a special night. Once she had said yes, he called Caleb to drive them. When they arrived at the hotel, Caleb said he had to go into Towanda, and he would be back in about two hours.

Once they had placed their orders, they started talking about Jacob's work. "I have wanted to talk to you about my work for some time," he said. "My work is going really well. Dad and I have so many orders that we will probably have to hire more help. That Miller job in Owego has netted a great deal of money, to say nothing of the orders that we have received from it. I made out very well financially too. That is the reason I asked you to come tonight."

"Oh, no! You are not going away again, are you?" she asked.

"No, that's not it. I want to ask you if you will be my wife?"

Sally sat and stared at him for a minute, not sure she heard him right. "Did you asked me to marry you?"

"Yes, I did."

"My answer is yes. I have been in love with your since our first young people's get together."

Jacob reached across the table and put his hand on hers. "You have made me very happy."

They talked and laughed during their meal and planned their life together.

Jacob continued his work nonstop. When he wasn't in the shop working on their orders, he and Samuel were making kitchen cabinets for the new house. They also planned to make built-in cabinets for the bedrooms.

Sally told her parents about their dinner at the hotel in Wyalusing, and that Jacob has asked her to marry him, and she had said yes. They were very happy for them and relieved that Sally would have such a good, hardworking husband. They also talked about the date for the wedding. They wanted to do it the first Thursday in November, but they would have to make sure that that date was okay with the bishop.

"Where will you live?" her father asked a couple of months after they made their marriage plans known.

"We haven't discussed that," Sally replied.

"You are welcome to live in the Dawdi house if you like."

"I'll tell Jacob of your fine offer. Thank you."

About a week later, Jacob and Sally were sitting on the swing on Sally's front porch when she said, "My parents have offered us the Dawdi house to live in."

"Wow, we never even talked about where we will live. That would be great. When we go in, I'll thank them for their kind offer." A short time later, Jacob got up to leave. "I have a lot of work tomorrow. I guess I better get going."

"Okay, do you want to say goodbye to my parents?"

"Sure."

"I want to thank you for your offer for us to live in the Dawdi house. We really appreciate it," he said with a wink to her parents because they knew all about the house. Sally's father had even been over, helping with the construction.

Finally, November came, and Sally and Jacob were married. They had a wonderful day and were so happy. That night, they stayed at Sally's parents' house because of the cleanup the next day. Finally, when everything was back shipshape, Jacob said he wanted to go to visit his parents, so off they went in his buggy. Samuel had set a fire in the living room fireplace so the house would be warm when Jacob and Sally got there.

As they arrived at the King farm, Jacob turned in to the drive, but he didn't stop by the house; he kept going up the hill. "Where are we going?" Sally asked.

"I want to show you something first," Jacob said as he kept driving up the hill.

As they came around the slight bend in the road, the house came into view. "Look, someone has built a house up here. Who lives here?" she asked.

"We do. This is my wedding present to you."

She looked at Jacob with disbelief. "Our house? How did you keep it a secret? We have to tell my parents that we won't be using the Dawdi house."

"They already know. They have known about this for a long time, and your dad even helped in the construction."

The house was perfect for the newlyweds. It would be a good house for their future children to grow up in. Isn't it funny how history repeats itself? Jacob's father had done the same thing for his new bride many years ago, but that was something that Jacob did not know anything about.

As the years passed, Jacob's reputation grew. Samuel had turned the business over to him because of debilitating arthritis. Samuel would come into the shop and watch the men working, and Jacob knew that he wanted to work again, but it was just impossible. The business had grown so that they had put a big addition on the shop and now employed several Amish men to build the furniture.

One morning, as the men at the shop started the day's work, the bishop and three of the church deacons showed up. "Jacob, we need to talk to you."

"Let's step outside so we are not overheard," Jacob said, sensing that something was wrong.

"We see that your business is growing fast, and that you are employing more and more people all the time. Your business is pulling men who would be farmers into the work of business with the English. It has also come to our attention that you are now using some electric tools. This is not our way. You must reconsider this move and go back to using only propane-powered tools."

"I have provided a good deal of money to this community to help those who have been injured or who have had fires. I would not be able to do that if I was not a successful businessman."

"If you do not stop this now, you will be put under the shun. We will wait for your decision." And with that, they left.

Jacob was stunned. He could not believe their reaction. He decided that he needed to talk to Sally. She always had good suggestions and had a very logical mind. He told her about the conversation, and they talked for a long time. "This is my life's work. I have provided for my community as well as my family. I love being Amish. It is the only thing I know, but I will not be bullied into doing something that will slow my business down. How do you feel?"

"You are my husband and my life. I will go and do whatever you think is necessary."

As Jacob walked back to the shop, he thought about Jason Miller. I wonder if he still owns that warehouse where we had our shop when we were doing the work for him. Maybe I'll call him.

When he went into his office he immediately found Jason's card. He decided to call him right then. When the phone was answered in Owego, he asked to speak to Jason. "This is Jacob King. I did some work for him several years ago."

His secretary asked him to hold a moment.

"Jason Miller here. Is this my favorite woodworker?" he asked.

"It is Jacob King. How are you?"

"Fine. And you?"

"Well, I have a question. Do you remember when my dad and I did the work for you in that warehouse? Do you use that for your business, or is it possible to rent it?"

"It is so strange that you call about that now. My tenant just moved out. It is available, if you want it."

"First, I need to know how much the rent is?"

"For you, I will rent it to you for one thousand dollars a month. It has thirty thousand square feet of usable space."

"I'll take it," Jacob said. "When do you want me to come and sign the papers?"

"I'll hold it for you. When you start to move your equipment in, come and see me, and we'll get the legal stuff done."

Getting off the phone, Jacob went back to talk to Sally and tell her about the building for rent. "I will go back to the shop and have a meeting with our employees. I will give them the option to come with us or not."

"We will need a place to live. You wouldn't want to travel back and forth."

"Yes. We'll get a newspaper that has properties and apartments listed in it. We may have to live in an apartment for a while. Is that okay?" he asked.

"Of course, Jacob. Everything will be okay."

When Jacob went back to the shop, he got all the men to stop their work so he could talk to them. "I need to talk to you all. I have been forced to make a decision that I don't like very much, but here it is. The bishop and deacons came here this morning to talk to me. They are unhappy because we are now using machines that run by electricity. They told me that I either get rid of the electricity, or I will be shunned."

The men were shocked. They couldn't believe that the brethren would do that when Jacob had been so generous to the community.

"So in the few short hours since they left, I have made a decision. I will not be forced to ruin my business, so I have already rented a building in Owego, New York, to house our workshop. It is big enough for us to expand. But if you want to continue to work for me, you will have to relocate to Owego. It is too far to travel each day by buggy. You could hire someone to pick you up in the morning and then at night, but I want you all to know that you still have your jobs if you want them."

The next day, the bishop stopped by again. He said that he heard that Jacob was moving his business. "That is right, I will move my business, my life, and my family to Owego, New York. The shun is on. Good day, bishop."

And that is how Jacob and Sally came to be in Owego but still adhering to the Amish customs.

CHAPTER 10

Amos's Recovery

Amos's recovery took a little longer than he would have liked. It was a good thing that Mary had fixed up the Dawdi house for Jacob and Sally because they had been there several weeks. They loved the little house and really felt at home in Lancaster County.

Like the rest of the family from New York, Christine and Ken had to return home. Ken had work, and Christine had to get back to the children.

Jacob was in his glory, doing chores and repairs for Amos. He loved the work and felt more alive than he had in a long time. He loved the woodworking, but this work was invigorating. He knew that his business was in good hands back in Owego because he had a trustworthy foreman that was running everything.

Jacob had noticed a crack in one of the windows upstairs in the spare bedroom and decided that it would need to be fixed. He took the measurements and went and bought the glass to make the repair. He decided that he would replace the glass the next day when the sun would be out.

The next day dawned bright and sunny as he had hoped it would. It would be a good day to have the glass out and not get too cold. He carefully removed the cracked glass and was ready to put the new glass in when he noticed the corner of a piece of paper sticking out of a space in the wood trim of the window. He carefully pulled it out. He couldn't believe his eyes when he saw his name on the envelope. Was this some kind of a joke. Why would an envelope with his name on it be in the wall?

He decided to open it. As he started to read, it appeared to be an account of an event that happened years ago, and he was pretty sure that it had nothing to do with him. Yet he couldn't put it down, so he continued to read. First, it talked about the birth of a Jacob King Deitweller, son of Annie and Jacob Deitweller. Then it talked about a fire and the death of Jacob and how hard it was for Annie to function. She would just sit and stare. After the fire, Annie disappeared, but she left a letter to her sister and her husband Kate and Samuel Deitweller. Kate King married Annie's husband's brother Samuel. They had a daughter Rebecca Ruth who was born on February 12, the same day as Jacob King Deitweller.

Jacob's heart was beating fast. What did this mean? He continued to read. The letter Annie left for her sister said that she blamed Samuel for the fire that killed Annie's husband, Jacob, but asked them to take care of her son Jacob King Deitweller. Another tragedy came out of the fire. Samuel could not take the stress of everyday living in a house that looked out over the place where the barn was and where his brother died. He and Kate decided to pack up and move their little family away for a new start. They moved to Troy, Pennsylvania.

This can't be. His parents, Kate and Samuel, had the last name of King. He and Rebecca were twins, not cousins. What was the meaning of all this? Jacob continued to read.

In Troy, Kate and Samuel raised Jacob as their own. They told people that Rebecca and Jacob were twins to avoid questions and bringing up the fire.

Last they heard was that Samuel and Jacob had a very lucrative woodworking business. Samuel had retired, and Jacob had taken over to run it. Jacob married a nice Amish girl Sally Miller, and they lived in Troy with their daughter Elizabeth. Samuel and Kate never returned to the Strasburg area.

Annie finally returned to Strasburg many years later. She had remarried. Her husband was a man from Kinzers by the name of Jonathan Lapp. When they returned, they had their children with them. They had three boys Daniel, David, and Amos and a daughter Sarah. They still live in the area.

Jacob sat there. What did this mean? So he reread the paper. He was sitting on the floor with the paper in his hand when Sally came to check on him. "Jacob, what are you doing?" she asked.

"Sally, I don't know what to say," he said as he handed her the paper. "Read this."

Sally read and reread the pages just as Jacob had done. When she finished she looked at Jacob. "This means that Kate and Samuel were your aunt and uncle and not your parents, and that Annie is your mother, and your friend Amos is your half brother."

They sat on the floor of the upstairs bedroom for a long time, trying to digest all this information. Finally, Jacob stood up. "First, I need to put this glass back into the window and seal it. Then we will eat lunch. Then we will go and take this to Annie. She is the only one who can confirm or deny whether this is true or not."

Sally went downstairs to prepare lunch while Jacob put the glass back in the window. By the time he came down, she had sandwiches made and the soup heated. They sat and talked quietly about what they had just learned.

Once lunch was over and the dishes cleaned up, they headed to Annie and Jonathan's farm on Belmont Road. When they arrived at the Lapp farm, Annie came out to greet them. She was so happy to see them but knew that something was wrong when she saw their faces. "What is wrong?" she asked.

"Can we come in and sit down?" Jacob asked. "We have something to show you."

As they entered the kitchen, Annie said that she had just put on a pot of coffee and asked if they would like some.

"Is Jonathan here?"

"He is in the barn."

"I'll get him," Jacob said.

As he entered the barn, Jonathan was just finishing feeding the animals. "Hello, Jacob. Good to see you."

"Jonathan, can you come into the house?"

When the coffee was poured, and all were seated, Jacob asked, "Annie, are you my mother? I have found this letter of sorts, and it says that you are my mother, and that you left me with Kate and Samuel after my father died in a barn fire. Is that true?"

"Yes, I am. I'm not proud of that time in my life. I am sorry."

"You should read this," Jacob said as he handed the paper to Annie and Jonathan to read.

Sally and Jacob sipped their coffee while Annie and Jonathan read and reread the papers. Looking up from the papers, Annie had tears in her eyes.

"So that is all true?" Jacob asked.

"Yes, I'm not proud of what I did, but I was not a stable person. I could not take care of you. I knew that Kate and Samuel would love you and take care of you. When Jonathan and I finally returned, and I found out how successful you were, I didn't want to do anything to change your life."

"Tell me about the fire."

"Your father, Jacob, was helping your grandfather and Samuel bring in the bales of hay and stack them in the hayloft. When your grandfather left to get the next wagon of hay, Samuel came down the ladder from the loft. When he stepped down, a barn cat tripped him, and he knocked over a lantern. The barn immediately caught fire. The only way down from the loft was the wooden ladder that Samuel had just come down. That was one of the first things to catch fire. Your adoptive father, Samuel, and your grandfather tried to put the fire out, but it was too far gone. The fire department came, but it was too late for Jacob. He was dead. I just shut down. I did not talk, eat, or take care of you.

"The day of the funeral, I screamed at Samuel that it was his fault. I was not very nice to him. That night, I left. I put a note on the kitchen table at our house and walked away from everything and everyone.

"There was never a day that went by that I didn't think of you. I have always loved you. I just couldn't take care of you. When I came back and found out that Kate and Samuel had moved away, I did not want to disrupt your family, so I just kept quiet.

"The day of Amos's surgery was the day that I realized you might be my Jacob. Samuel, Amos's son, said at lunch he could not get over how much his father and you looked alike. That made me stop and think. And now I know that it is true. You are my son. I know that you probably can't forgive me, but I only did what I felt was best for you at the time."

"I think I can understand why you did it. I have heard about people being so consumed with grief that they can't function. I also understand why Kate and Samuel did what they did. I have had a good life, and I owe that to them. They were wonderful parents to me.

"I can forgive you. I don't know what it would be like to lose the person that you loved almost more than life itself. I am just glad that we finally found each other. What a family reunion this has been. Our long-lost grandson that was kidnapped ends up being truly related to the people that adopted him. Now that's amazing.

"So let's see. Amos is my half brother? I can't wait to tell him. That is why we felt such a bond. Doesn't God work in mysterious ways? If Amos hadn't gotten sick, and we hadn't stayed, we probably would have never known."

"Hey, does Amos know about me?"

"No. Jonathan and my family are the only ones that know."

"Let's go tell him."

As the men headed out to hitch up the buggies, the women sat in the quiet for a few minutes. Annie finally said, "I can't believe that he is so forgiving."

"That is the way Jacob has always been."

Amos was sitting on the porch as the buggies pulled into the drive. While Jonathan and Jacob tied the horses to the hitching post, Annie and Sally made their way to the porch. As Annie and Sally went up the porch steps, Annie asked Amos where they could find Mary?

"She is in the kitchen."

Mary came out on the porch then. "What's going on? Is something wrong?" Amos asked.

Jacob started. "This morning, I was replacing a broken window in the Dawdi house and found an envelope with my name on it. It has to do with your family, so I went to your parents first, and now we're here to show you this," he said as he pulled the envelope out of his pocket. He handed it to Mary and Amos and asked them to read it.

Once they had read it and then read it again, Amos looked up and asked, "This means that you are my half brother."

"Yes, it does."

Amos looked with questions in his eyes.

"I was ashamed that I wasn't mentally sound enough to take care of my own child. When we came back to Strasburg and found out that Jacob was a successful businessman, I didn't want to interfere in his life, so I didn't say anything. I know now that that was wrong. Amos, I also ask for your forgiveness as I have asked for Jacob's."

"There is nothing to forgive. We have found each other now, and that is all that is important. My brother, how about that."

"What was my father like?" Jacob asked.

"He was a wonderful man, and I had loved him from the time I entered school. He worked hard and played hard, and when we were getting ready to get married, he built me the most beautiful house for a wedding present."

Jacob looked at Sally, and they both started laughing.

"What did I say that is so funny?" Annie asked.

"My Jacob did the same thing. It was a surprise. I didn't know anything about it until the day after our wedding and he took me there."

"Jacob, you are so like your father. He too was a wood worker. He would help around the farm when he could, and that is what he was doing the day of the fire."

The small group sat for several hours talking, asking questions, and hearing more about Jacob. They were amazed at how big his business was, and that he continued to grow. They asked about his and Sally's still sticking to the old ways and why. Finally, Mary said, "I think we need to get some food on the table." So the women left the men on the porch talking.

Once the meal was prepared, everyone sat down to a family meal together. When Amos and Mary's children started coming in, they were surprised to see everyone at the table. "What's going on here, a party?" they asked.

"Today has been a day of revelations," Amos said. "Today we have found a family member that we didn't know existed. I will tell you all that I know, and then your grandmother can fill in anything I left out.

"A number of years ago, there was a fire, and a young husband and father lost his life. His wife was so distraught that she could not take care of herself, let alone her young son. Her husband died while he has helping his father and brother put hay away. A lantern got knocked over, and the fire ignited immediately, and the barn was totally engulfed in flames. The ladder to the hayloft burned, and the young man was trapped up there. That is how he died. He left a young son and his wife. The wife just could not live without her husband, so she left a note and walked away from all her family and friends in the Lancaster area.

"Years later, when she was able to come to grips with what happened, she returned to the Strasburg area with her new husband and four children from that marriage. It took my having an appendicitis to bring the mother and son back together again. Mom, have I pretty much covered everything?"

"Yes, son. I hope that you all can forgive me for leaving my son and starting over. I was not fit mentally to take care of him. The son that I left with my sister and her husband is Jacob. He is my son. So that means that Jacob and Amos are half brothers. He is your uncle."

When the story had been told, Samuel piped up and said, "I told grandmother the day you were in surgery that I thought that you and Jacob looked enough alike to be brothers, didn't I?"

Annie said, "Yes, you did, and it was what made me start thinking that maybe it was possible that he could be my Jacob. I am truly blessed to have all my children now."

For several hours, they sat around the table drinking coffee and eating shoofly pie and talked about the turn of events that turned Jacob from Daniel's grandfather and a friend of the family to a full blown member of the family. Finally, Daniel spoke up and said, "I don't know whether I should call Jacob grandfather or uncle."

Everyone laughed. The family, together, decided that the rest of the members of the family should know the story. It was something that was going to be hard to do; but together, it would all work out. It was decided that there would be a family get together with all of Amos's children and their families and Annie's children and their families. "It would be wonderful if Kate and Samuel could come too," Annie said. "Maybe I will write them a letter to see if they could possibly come down. I will pay for their transportation if they can."

Jacob and Sally said that they would call the family in New York and ask them if they could all come down because there was to be a family get together, and they needed to be down here for it.

So the wheels were turning, and the planning would start in earnest the next day. They wanted to have the get together in two weeks. That would give everyone plenty of time to make all the arrangements to come. It was also an off weekend for church, so they could be together for two days.

For the next two weeks, the women cooked, and the men did the cleanup work around the farm. The barn would need to be cleaned so they could set up tables in there for them to eat at. The men put new hay on the floor of the barn, and it was almost as clean as the house. The women had prepared plenty of food and had put most of it into the freezers.

On Friday, Ken and Caroline arrived in Strasburg with Alyssa and Trent, followed soon by James and Elizabeth and Dan and Carol Ann. Once they had gotten settled at the inn, they all went to the Lapp farm. When they arrived, it was a flurry of activity. As hard as they tried to find out what was going on, no one would tell them anything, except that they would have to wait until tomorrow.

Finally came the day for the family get together. The group from New York met more people that they had not met before. The women were busy getting the food out to the barn and ready for the meal. Everyone was seated and ready to start eating. Once the silent prayer was said, everyone ate to their heart's content.

Then it was time to disclose the information about a new member of the family. Amos stood up and got everyone's attention. "I know that you are all wondering why this family get together. It has come to our attention that a number of years ago, a family member was lost."

As he was saying this, the barn door opened, and there stood Kate and Samuel. "Father, I can't believe that you have been able to come down," Jacob said. And then there was a flurry of activity to get them seated and fed before Amos continued.

Once they had finished eating and were getting acquainted with everyone again, Amos stood up again to finish the disclosure. "Now, as I saying, back a number of years ago, there was a family tragedy. A young man lost his life in a barn fire and left his wife and son alone. The wife was so distressed that she could not deal with the loss of her husband. She left a note on the kitchen table, asking her sister and her husband to take care of her son.

"They did just that. He was raised as their own child and never knew that they were not his true parents. That is, until a couple of weeks ago when he found a document that had the full story. Now I know that you are wondering who that little boy is? Well, it is Jacob King. His name is actually Jacob King Deitweller, and his parents were Jacob and Annie Deitweller.

"I want to also say that Kate and Samuel took over raising Jacob for Annie, and they have done a wonderful job. We are so thankful for them. Now I think my mother wants to say something."

"I know that you may be thinking, 'How could a mother just walk away from her son?' You have to understand that I was not in my right mind when the fire happened. I just could not function. I left, and for years I never looked back.

"Then I met a wonderful man who became my second husband. And together, we have worked through the event. I am so thankful to Kate and Samuel for their love and nurturing that they have shown Jacob all these years. I also ask their forgiveness for the horrible things I said at the time of the fire."

Amos stood again and spoke, "This all started because a family in New York was looking for their kidnapped son, and has ended with the fact that the child that was kidnapped, Daniel, actually was raised by a family member after all. When Daniel's family came down from New York several months ago, Mary and I felt such a bond with Jacob and Sally that we could not understand. But now we know why that bond was so strong. He is my brother, and we love him."

It took everyone a while to comprehend what they had just been told. It was a story that started in tragedy and ended with a reunion of a loving family. The family continued to sit around the table and visited for a long time after. Daniel had found his biological parents, and Amos and Jacob found a new family for all.

Sometimes, we don't understand why things happen the way they do, but it is God's plan, not ours. It is important that we learn to put our trust and faith in him.

The end!

About the Author

Nancy grew up in Upstate New York in the village of Endicott. It is located about fifteen miles east of Owego, New York, which is mentioned in the book. She and her husband, Lynn, have two daughters who are married with families of their own. Nancy now lives east of Atlanta, Georgia.

She wrote *Finding Daniel* because she had this story in her head for a number of years and decided to put it down on paper. Over the years, Nancy and her family have spent many hours in the land of the Amish in Pennsylvania and Ohio. She has enjoyed learning about their lifestyle and how their daily life is different than hers.

CPSIA information can be obtained
at www.ICGtesting.com
Printed in the USA
LVHW021523270620
659107LV00003B/578

9 781646 706501